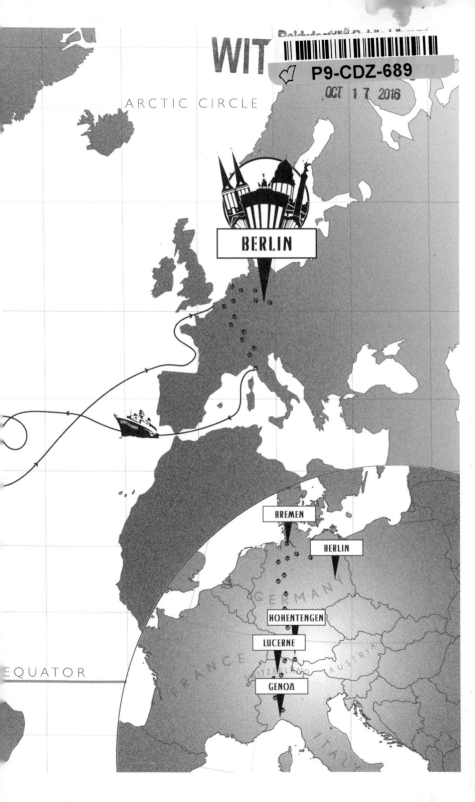

WIT

ARCTIC CIRCLE

BERLIN

BREMEN

BERLIN

HOHENTENGEN

LUCERNE

EQUATOR

GENOA

SIRIUS

**A NOVEL ABOUT THE LITTLE DOG
WHO ALMOST CHANGED HISTORY**

JONATHAN CROWN

Translated from German by Jamie Searle Romanelli

Scribner

New York   London   Toronto   Sydney   New Delhi

Scribner
An Imprint of Simon & Schuster, Inc.
1230 Avenue of the Americas
New York, NY 10020

First Scribner hardcover edition October 2016

SCRIBNER and design are registered trademarks of The Gale Group, Inc., used under license by Simon & Schuster, Inc., the publisher of this work.

For information about special discounts for bulk purchases, please contact Simon & Schuster Special Sales at 1-866-506-1949 or business@simonandschuster.com.

The Simon & Schuster Speakers Bureau can bring authors to your live event. For more information or to book an event, contact the Simon & Schuster Speakers Bureau at 1-866-248-3049 or visit our website at www.simonspeakers.com.

Endpaper and interior illustrations by Pascal Blanchet

Manufactured in the United States of America

1 3 5 7 9 10 8 6 4 2

Library of Congress Cataloging-in-Publication Data is available.

ISBN 978-1-5011-4499-8
ISBN 978-1-5011-4501-8 (ebook)

For my family, who lived in Berlin
during that period

PART 1

EVERY MORNING, at ten o'clock on the dot, Professor Liliencron steps out of his house, and what happens next is always the same: he draws in a deep breath of air, as if he were standing on a mountaintop in the Alps, drinking in the healthy climate. Even his clothes are suggestive of this wanderlust: a flat cap, a hiking jacket, knee breeches. Next to him, ready and waiting, is his fox terrier. The dog waves his tail expectantly, thinking, "Now we're off!" Then the two of them trot down Klamtstrasse, a small side street just off Berlin's Kurfürstendamm. At the first tree, they stop. The dog snuffles around. Herr Liliencron pulls a book out of his jacket pocket and reads. Nothing disturbs their tranquillity. Neighbors call out their greetings. Herr Liliencron nods back in a friendly fashion, then immerses himself in his book once more. Meanwhile, the dog circles the tree, as swiftly as he can, his snout always right up next to the trunk, where a few blades of grass grow. Sometimes he barks at the tree, growling invitingly, as if he wants to play with it. Then he lifts his leg.

This can continue for a good half hour. Eventually, Herr Liliencron claps his book shut, puts it away in his pocket and

prepares to set off back home. The dog has no such inten-
tions. He wants to play with the tree for longer, *much* longer.
Herr Liliencron calls his name, softly but sternly: "Levi!"

Levi knows that he is the one being addressed. Every
single time this happens, he tries to put on an expression
which—in his opinion, at least—can't fail to have a heart-
wrenching impact. He accompanies this with a pitiful yelp,
drooping his tail and nestling up close to the tree as a gesture
of deeply felt inseparability.

Herr Liliencron begins to head off. As he walks away, he
casually unwraps a bar of chocolate, as if it were mere coincidence that he should do so at this moment. The crackle of
the paper wrapping weakens Levi's resolve. The tree will
still be there tomorrow, he thinks to himself. Transitory
things should always take precedence.

The professor and his dog. Always at the same time,
always at the same tree. In the heart of Berlin.

*

The Liliencron family live in a grand town house, which the
Leopoldina—the German National Academy of Sciences—
has put at the disposal of its honorary member.

Professor Carl Liliencron has held this role since he was
awarded with the golden Cothenius Medal. Soon after, he
moved into the stately residence with his wife, Rahel, and
their two children, Georg and Else.

"This house needs a dog," he declared ceremoniously.
And that was how Levi came into their lives.

* * *

Now it is spring. In the year 1938.

In the long history of the Leopoldina, Carl Liliencron is its youngest dignitary. Forty-two years young. And yet his hair is already white, sticking up erratically from the sides of his balding pate in a manner befitting of the bearer of the Cothenius Medal. Sometimes, nature knows in advance what the world has in store for someone.

Liliencron's subject is microscopy. At his institute, he researches the relationships between Arctic and Antarctic plankton.

"Anything bigger than ten thousandths of an inch is of no interest to me," he is fond of saying.

This is also how he explains his disinterest in Adolf Hitler. And politics. And the future. His opinion on these things is that they are "all too big."

And this man, of all people, who declares everything visible to the naked eye to be inconsequential, has a wife whose beauty cannot fail to be seen at the very first glance. Isn't that strange?

Rahel's beauty has long been the talk of Berlin. She had famous suitors, like Wilhelm Furtwängel and Peter Lorre. But she chose the man with the microscope. "He sees the unseeable. That's such a hoot, don't you think?"

Rahel Liliencron takes a cheerful approach to life. First thing in the morning, while she gets dressed and does her hair, joyful music already pours out from the gramophone. Records that are all the rage in the dance halls of Berlin.

"Come on, Carl," she says to her husband. "Dance with

me!" He shakes his head. Too young for the Cothenius Medal, too old for the here and now, he thinks. It's odd, really.

Sometimes, though, he does dance with her.

Rahel loves fashion. Her sister, who lives in Paris, sends her the latest couture magazines. Rahel then has the clothes made. And quickly! She wants to be the first in Berlin to cause a stir with the season's newest trends.

To this day, Rahel still doesn't know exactly what plankton are. "But the most important thing is that *you* know," she says to Carl.

She shows him a pink outfit the seamstress has just finished for her. A Coco Chanel design. "I bet your plankton can't do this."

"That's where you're mistaken, my love," answers Carl. "The green algae adapt their shading every season. According to the wavelength of the light absorbed through their membranes." He smiles lovingly. "I'm quoting from my definitive reference work *Phytoplankton and Photosynthesis*. You can read up on it there."

Rahel knows the book. It's one of the weighty tomes she fetches from the library while Carl is in the institute during the day. She piles the books up on top of one another on the floor. "Levi," she calls. "Time to play. Come on, up we go!"

Levi is a clever dog. After three or four attempts he knows what's being asked of him. Sometimes he jumps over the obstacle, sometimes he enthrones himself on it and plays "sit up and beg."

Or, at the command "Levi, read!" he acts as though he is

leafing through the book with his paws. Then he slumps theatrically, closes his eyes and snores.

He loves these little performances.

In the late afternoon, Carl often comes back home with a few colleagues from the academy. They retreat to the library, drink cognac and discuss work matters. Professor Hertz is there, the Nobel Prize laureate for physics, and Rafael Honigstein, the famous paleontologist. Recently, their conversations have had a tendency to stray away from the natural sciences and toward politics instead. The Nuremberg Laws. The book burning. The harassment of Jewish academics and students. These are bleak times. What can be done?

Levi listens attentively.

Soon, the moment comes in which Liliencron paces over to the bookshelves and, with a furious flourish, holds *Mein Kampf* up in the air.

Levi gets to his feet, barks several times as loud as he can, then extends his right paw up high in a Hitler salute. Another trick that Rahel has taught him.

The academic gathering applauds. They also know that this is the signal: it is time for them to head home.

"You still need to teach him to do his business on that book," says Carl to his wife, who accompanies the guests to the door.

Evenings in the Liliencron house are dedicated to the family.

Putti, their Swiss maid, serves dinner in the conservatory. Later, Else gives a short concert on the piano.

"She has talent," the conductor Fritz Mahler once said. He is a friend of the family, and on occasion used to accompany Else on the piano. "But I doubt very much that it would be to our Führer's liking."

Mahler emigrated to New York two years ago, and wanted to take Else with him. But her parents thought she was too young. She was thirteen at the time.

The black Bechstein piano stands in the salon. Else is playing the second movement of Schubert's Sonata in B-flat Major. A melancholy andante which becomes increasingly delicate, fading more and more, until only the hint of a touch brushes the keys. All of a sudden, the mighty piano is whispering tones which are almost inaudible.

Else seems to be drowning in the music. Her red hair tumbles down onto the keys in waves, her pale skin is reflected in the surface of the piano as if in a deep, dark ocean. The last accord: *Death and the Maiden*.

At this moment, Else feels the impatience of her heart. The longing for her first great love. When will it finally come?

Georg is her older brother. He will soon be sitting his final exams at the Fichte Gymnasium. He is the last "non-Aryan" student in his year group. He wants to become a doctor, but Jewish students are prohibited from going to university.

Father Liliencron remains steadfast: "Sauerbruch promised to put in a good word for you, remember."

By the age of six, Georg was already dissecting cats; the skulls of the little creatures, preserved in formalin, still stand on his desk to this day.

He always wears a suit and tie to school. By the time he gets home, his clothes are often tattered. "Self-defense" is his usual comment, accompanied by a shrug of the shoulders. He smiles wickedly at the thought of the blows his attackers had to take in return.

Georg is a member of the East Berlin Sports Association. His trainer is Werner Seelenbinder, the German light heavyweight wrestling champion, who refused to do the Hitler salute on the winner's podium at the 1936 Olympic Games.

Refusal? Resistance? Resignation? Flight?

Georg's thoughts are going around in circles, and the circles keep getting smaller and smaller. He knows there isn't much time left. The future, this unpredictable monster, is marching toward the Liliencrons with its flag brandished in the air—and then what?

"Look at that sky!" calls Rahel, stepping out onto the terrace. "So starry and clear."

The Liliencron family gathers beneath the firmament. There is a new moon. "Look, there's Sirius," says Father Liliencron with delight. "Do you see?"

His finger points up into the darkness, to where light is still burning at the end of the universe.

"The constellation is called *Big Dog*."

Levi lifts his head. His gaze follows the finger into the black night. *Big Dog*. He suddenly feels sad, thinking back to the day when he was small. Very small.

*

Back when the Liliencrons were on the lookout for a suitable dog, the dachshund Kuno von Schwertberg—Kurwenal for short—was making headlines.

He belonged to Mathilde Freiin von Freytag-Loringhoven, an exponent of New Animal Psychology in Weimar.

Kurwenal was able to read and converse. He expressed himself by barking the exact number of times to correspond with the consecutively numbered alphabet.

The famous animal psychologist William McKenzie made the journey especially from Genoa and held his business card under the dog's nose. Kurwenal read it and then barked: "Magnzi" and "Gnoa." He was following the phonetic alphabet, of course.

McKenzie set off on his journey home, enthralled.

Two British researchers visited Kurwenal and surprised him by asking what they were wearing on their heads. Kurwenal promptly answered: "Fancy hats."

It wasn't long before a delegation of the National Socialist Animal Protection Association took an interest in the brilliant dachshund, although admittedly with sinister ulterior motives. If speaking and thinking animals existed, then humans—like Jews, Gypsies and Poles—could be speaking and thinking animals too. In other words, *Untermenschen*, subhumans.

All of this brought a plan to Isidor Reich's mind.

Isidor Reich was a young, up-and-coming zoologist, who no longer wanted to stand by and watch new comparative psychology risk ending up in the hands of the National Socialists. He came up with the idea of a "Jewish Kurwenal." And that was how he began breeding fox terriers in Berlin's Grunewald district.

His dogs' pedigree wasn't made up of pompous aristocratic titles like Kuno von Schwertberg, but Jewish forenames, in alphabetical order, accompanied by the litter number and breeding name *Reich*.

The first Reich consisted of five puppies, named Ariel, Benjamin, Chajm, David and Esther. Reich selected the dog that seemed the most eager to learn, Benjamin, and subjected him to obsessive schooling from that moment on.

From early in the morning until late at night, the dog sat at the typewriter and obediently typed out with his paw the letters Reich called out to him. After a year had passed, Benjamin was capable of transcribing a report dictated to him without any problems whatsoever.

Meanwhile, the second Reich had been whelped. Gidon, Hadassah, Irit and Jakob. This time, Jakob was the most gifted. He was without a doubt Benjamin's son, and that's why it was no great surprise—or perhaps it was, when you really think about it—that Jakob had writing in his blood. At the age of six months, he composed his first and very own poem.

cad a baf
bdd af dff
art ad
abd ad arrli
bed a ccat

The verse was published in *Animal Souls*, the journal of new comparative psychology. It was a triumph.

Then the third Reich came into the world: Levi, Mirjam, Natan, Oz and Ruth.

But that was the end already. One morning, the Gestapo broke down the door, and Isidor Reich was arrested and deported. All the dogs were shot dead.

All apart from one. Little Levi.

He made his way to safety just in the nick of time. A neighbor found the trembling bundle of fur at the farthermost end of the kitchen, where presumably he had been mistaken for a pillow.

The only survivor of the third Reich. Back then, Levi had no idea that what he had escaped was only the beginning of the hell to come.

*

Professor Liliencron never reads the newspapers. Not under normal circumstances, that is. His curiosity is predominantly piqued by living things which are 3.5 billion years old. And they are rarely mentioned in the newspapers, so as far as he was concerned it wasn't worth reading them.

Today, though, he is reading the papers.

He sits at the breakfast table. Still in his dressing gown. His walk with Levi, at ten o'clock on the dot, has been waived today. Instead, Putti took the dog out and fetched the freshly baked rolls.

Rahel trembles as she pours the coffee. She knows her husband only reads the papers when bad forebodings make it absolutely necessary.

"News!" says Father Liliencron. "Interesting news. And I'm afraid it concerns us."

"What is it?" asks Else.

He reads out loud: "The second decree for the implementation of the law of August 17, 1938, regarding the alteration of surnames and forenames."

He imitates the officious tone of a reading before a court of law.

"Paragraph 1. Jews are only permitted to bear such forenames as are listed in the guidelines set out by the Reich Minister of the Interior."

He slams his fist down thunderously on the table.

"Anyone who deliberately disobeys this order will be sentenced to up to six months imprisonment."

The noise wakes Levi. He was slumbering contentedly on his dog blanket under the table. Normally he is awoken gently from his dreams, perhaps by the scent of a slice of cheese being proffered to him, in order that he feel like a fully fledged member of the breakfast gathering. But today is not a normal day.

Has he done something wrong? Is the commotion about *him*? He articulates his uncertainty with a low whimper.

"Does the law apply to dogs too?" asks Else. "Does Levi need to change his forename?"

"It wouldn't surprise me one bit!" responds Father Liliencron bitterly, putting on his gold-rimmed reading glasses. "Let's read the small print."

The family looks at him expectantly.

"Terrible," he murmurs. "We need to start watching our backs."

"Start?" asks Georg sarcastically. "I've been watching mine for a long time now."

"I know"—Liliencron nods—"I know. But unfortunately we can't pick and choose the times we live in."

"Well, you did," retorts Georg. "You live in the past."

Rahel interrupts: "Leave your father be, Georg."

Levi clears his throat, drawing attention to himself.

Liliencron leans down toward him. "You don't understand any of this. Or do you?"

Levi sits up and sways his head wistfully back and forth in rhythm with the hand stroking him.

"It's too dangerous out there if you have a Jewish name," Liliencron explains to his dog.

He lays the newspaper aside and gets up.

"That's why, as of this moment, you will no longer be called Levi!" he declares. Levi furrows his brow.

"We'll find a beautiful new name for you," says Liliencron. "Then you can give the Aryans the runaround."

He closes his eyes and thinks. Big Dog. The constellation pops into his mind. The evening on the terrace. His dog has grown pretty big by now, hasn't he?

"Sirius!" The name suddenly bursts out of him.

He stares into the startled faces of his family.

"Sirius!" he repeats ceremoniously. "From this moment on, you will be called Sirius."

Levi feels flattered. Big Dog. But at the same time he feels the responsibility weighing down on both himself and the star— of being a glimmer of light in the darkness. Dogs called Rusty have an easier ride of it.

"Sirius, come on!"

Liliencron grabs the lead, and together they leave the house.

The passersby can't believe their eyes. The professor, still in his dressing gown and at a much later hour than usual, is walking absentmindedly along the street. And he's calling his dog "Sirius."

"Sirius, let's go!"

Frau Zinke, the wife of the caretaker from the neighboring building, who sometimes makes conversation with the professor on his morning walks, asks: "Isn't that Levi?"

Liliencron answers: "No, that's our Sirius."

Sirius trots on ahead, his ears drooping. When he reaches the tree, his tree, he doesn't bark, but instead lies down thoughtfully.

"Is it a different dog?" asks Frau Zinke.

"Yes and no," replies Liliencron.

Frau Zinke shakes her head in bewilderment.

*

The town house the Liliencrons live in is an imposing structure.

The entrance is framed by two columns, and the door is crowned with a frieze, modeled on the famous ceiling scene in the Sistine Chapel, Michelangelo's *The Creation of Adam*.

The story goes that the building's architect, a certain Manfred Buonarroti, was a descendent of Michelangelo who opened an architectural firm in Berlin in the mid-nineteenth century. Liliencron researched the story, but was unable to find proof of the genealogical line from Michelangelo to Manfred. All he found was mention of a sculptor called Manfred Hosemann, from Leipzig, who once spent a month in Florence in 1821.

There is another unmissable reference to Michelangelo in the conservatory: a statue of David in miniature incorporated into a niche in the wall. "Ecce homo" is engraved beneath it.

For some time now, Liliencron has been contemplating replacing the David with a bust of his dog. The plan cheers him up. The inscription "Ecce homo" would of course remain, he thinks to himself.

By now a few weeks have passed, and Sirius has accepted his new identity. He has almost forgotten that he was once called Levi. So quickly.

"Presumably Hitler has also long forgotten that he was once called Schicklgruber," says Liliencron.

Frau Zinke has certainly forgotten, in any case. She calls "Hello, Sirius!" when she sees the dog. And "*Heil Hitler!*" when she sees Herr Liliencron.

Life goes on nonetheless. Every morning, at ten o'clock on the dot, Professor Liliencron steps out of his house, followed by Sirius, and together they walk down Klamtstrasse.

When they get to the corner, the dog begins his ritual with the tree, and Liliencron reads his book.

The chocolate, which was once a trick to lure the dog home, is no longer necessary. Sirius knows the route now. He knows the whole neighborhood.

Sometimes he even ventures out on his own.

He has discovered a hole in the garden fence, and he's off. His first stop is Café Hoffmann on Clausewitzstrasse. He takes up position expectantly before the door, barks and wags his tail.

"Right then, let's see if you've learned any new tricks," says Herr Hoffmann.

Sirius sits up and begs.

"What? That's it?" Herr Hoffmann acts disappointed. "That's all you've got?"

Sirius jumps into the air, somersaults—and lands on his front paws.

"Now that's a lot better, isn't it!" praises Herr Hoffmann, taking out a nut triangle.

Now it's Sirius's turn to express his disappointment. He droops his ears theatrically, acting as though he is about to slink away dejectedly.

"Okay then," says Herr Hoffmann. "Two nut triangles."

Sirius barks joyfully, grabs his reward and sets off on his way. He struts curiously down Kantstrasse. He isn't quite bold enough to venture down the Ku'damm just yet.

"Good day to you, Sirius!" cries the bookseller Friedrich in greeting, raising his hat.

At Savignyplatz, Sirius lies down on a park bench in the sun and dozes. Later, he trots toward Fasanenstrasse, where two garbagemen are in the process of pushing two rattling dumpsters across the cobbles.

"Hey, we know him!" cries one as they catch sight of Sirius. "That Jew dog belongs in with the rubbish!"

They take pleasure in frightening him with their wild facial expressions and threatening gesticulations.

Sirius is an intrepid dog. His shaggy fur, mottled white, brown and black, gives him a rebellious, belligerent air.

He looks like a dusty carpet that inspired the tricolor of some unknown land.

Perhaps it was No-Man's-Land.

*

Berlin, the city of gray, stumbles toward summer like a prisoner finally released from his sad cell, praising God that he is able to see the blue sky again after so long. Hungry for sunshine. Greedy for exercise. Gasping for fresh air. Thirsty for beer.

On Father's Day, grown men hoot as they set off into the

countryside in their automobiles, grilling and fishing equip-
ment in tow. Summer, at last!

The bars set up tables outside on the terraces. The people are
clothed in the bare minimum of attire. The pavements
become the stage of a vast, summery open-air theater. At the
weekends, everyone flocks to the Wannsee beach.

    This is the unique spirit of Berlin. Even in the summer of
1938.

Out of necessity, the Liliencron family have weaned themselves off their longing for the great outdoors. Most aspects
of public life are now forbidden for Jews, who have to make
do with the pleasure provided by their own gardens. Now
and then, Liliencron still takes his automobile out of the
garage, his beloved Mercedes 170 V convertible, and invites
the others to join him for a quick jaunt around Grunewald.
But the resentful looks spoil their fun.

Georg passes his finals with flying colors. After the celebration at the gymnasium, the whole family gathers around the
large marble table out on the terrace.

    Putti looks particularly fetching; for special occasions she
exchanges her white cook's apron for a dress, one that also
happens to flaunt her impressive décolletage. Her little Swiss
cheeks are glowing even after the first glass of champagne.

    Benno Fritsche, Georg's godfather, is practically part of
the family. He is a well-known personality in Berlin. An actor
at the Deutsches Theater, and star of the film *Grindelhof*,
which has just started its run in cinemas. He plays, once

again, a devastatingly handsome heartbreaker who has women throwing themselves at his feet.

Fritsche loves to make a grand entrance. Imitating the fanfare of a circus trumpet, he jumps over the low garden fence. He lives in the villa right next door, and they have been neighbors ever since the Liliencrons moved into their town house.

"As you can see, I wasn't afraid to take the long way around!" he calls out in greeting.

Rahel puts on her most charming smile. The blush on Putti's cheeks is reminiscent of the glow of the Alps in her homeland. Even Else seems spellbound.

Benno Fritsche is a delicate subject.

First of all, there's his hair. When Benno contentedly brushes his blond bangs back off his forehead with both hands, as he does frequently, it makes the balding Liliencron feel anxious.

The fact that Rahel seems transformed in Benno's presence doesn't make matters any easier. She starts to flirt like a young girl. All Benno has to do is make some witty remark, and Rahel just melts.

But the biggest issue is this: Benno has joined the Nazi Party.

Involuntarily, he assures them. That's how things are in the movie business, he says: no Party membership, no work. But then there's the fact that he recently had an article published in the *Völkischer Beobachter*, the NSDAP newspaper, entitled "The Aryan Art of Acting." Did he really need to do that?

* * *

Carl expressed great doubt as to whether Fritsche should even be invited to the celebration.

"He's Georg's godfather!" said Rahel sternly. "Carl, don't be so jealous."

"He's a Nazi!" Carl retorted.

To which Rahel replied: "He's not a Nazi. He's an actor. He's playing the role of a Nazi so that he can continue being an actor. All of us are wearing masks nowadays. Even Sirius."

Liliencron reluctantly gave in.

So there he sits at the table, Uncle Benno.

Father Liliencron lifts his glass. "My dear Georg Israel," he says, beginning his speech.

Not a great start, thinks Rahel, flinching a little. But it's correct; this is now her son's official name, according to the guidelines of the Reich Minister for Internal Affairs. Jewish men have to add the forename Israel, and Jewish women the name Sara. But was this really the time and the place to use it?

Uncle Benno doesn't bat an eyelash.

Carl goes on to give a witty speech, which pays tribute to Georg's life so far, singling out defining moments and poignant anecdotes, and of course he is unable to resist making a sweeping diversion to the subject of plankton.

Carl turns to Rahel and recounts their wonderful love story once more. He pays tribute to Else. He recalls how the lovely Putti came into their lives, as a souvenir from their winter holiday in Arosa, where she made a lasting impression as the waitress in Hotel Kulm.

Tears of emotion stream down their faces, which moves the orator to include even Uncle Benno and commemorate their childhood friendship.

Benno uses both hands to sweep his bangs from his forehead. Then the speech draws to an end.

"And now to you, little Sirius!"

The dog is sitting on Else's lap, and has been listening attentively the whole time.

"Sirius?" whispers Benno, shooting Else a questioning glance. The renaming has so far escaped him.

"Yes, Sirius," says Liliencron. "That's his name now. We all have new names, so the dog does too. Everyone has a mask in these macabre times."

Rahel smiles back meaningfully.

Liliencron had actually been planning to close with an observation that would serve as an emotive proclamation for the principles of humanism. He wanted to glance at Sirius and say: We are not animals to be divided into races, we are people. What gives you so-called Aryans the right to take the lives of us Jews? We are Germans. Just like you.

But suddenly, he can't find the words. He simply looks at Sirius and says:

"You are a *big dog*."

Else is in love. Her crush is named Andreas Cohn, and he is one of her fellow students at the Hollaender Jewish Private School of Music. She plays the piano, he the violin.

They used to be in the same class at the Stern Conservatory, which three years ago was renamed and Aryanized as the Conservatory of the Reich Capital of Berlin. Numerous Jewish professors had to leave the school. After that, Kurt Hollaender founded his private music academy on Sybelstrasse.

Else and Andreas became closer while they were rehearsing Felix Mendelssohn Bartholdy's Violin Concerto, op. 64, arranged for violin and piano.

Erich Oppenheimer, the piano teacher, said: "Fräulein Else, you have to play the first movement as though your heart has just caught fire. The second movement is when the heart hesitantly withdraws and ponders: does he feel the same way? The third movement is, finally, the fulfillment of that great love."

If you look at it like this, Else is currently in the middle of the second movement of her first great love.

Andreas is a serious young man. His curly black hair and deep-set eyes give him a defiant air. He plays the violin with a smoldering, almost fear-inducing fervor. He braces his instrument, a Stainer, against his shoulder like a crossbow, as if he were a marksman about to fire the deciding arrow. A fighter. A daredevil.

Else, by contrast, seems like his guardian angel. She could almost have jumped straight out of a Raphael painting. Graceful, sweet and gentle.

They wait for each other after class. Until the corner of Mommsenstrasse, their journey home is the same, and sometimes they sit there on a bench for hours, because they cannot bear to be parted.

* * *

"What do you see when you close your eyes?" asks Else.

Andreas closes his eyes. "I see the Rhine. Imagine how small it is when it flows out of the Tomasee lake up in the mountains. A tiny little stream. In the Romansh language, the source of the Rhine is called *Lai da Tuma*. *Tuma* means 'grave.'"

Else hangs on to his every word.

He opens his eyes again. "By the time the Rhine flows past us here, it's already a vast, broad river."

Andreas Cohn is from Basel. His grandfather Arthur Cohn was the first rabbi of the Israelite congregation in Basel, where Theodor Herzl later founded the dream of a Jewish state in Palestine.

"Take me with you, to Lai da Tuma," whispers Else. Andreas smiles. Then they kiss for the first time.

*

In the Liliencron household, Friday means soirée night. This week, the actor Erwin Kaltenberg has been invited. Along with Professor Weidenfels, the mathematician. Hans Fallada, the writer. Käthe Kollwitz, the artist. Arthur and Betty Fraenkel, the neighbors. And Else has invited Andreas along too.

"Be nice to him, Papa, okay?" she pleads.

"I'm sure we'll get along wonderfully," says Liliencron. "Assuming he has an interest in plankton, that is."

The guests trickle in.

Weidenfels swiftly commits a faux pas when he engages

Käthe Kollwitz in a conversation about dolls. He has confused her with Käthe Kruse, the famous doll maker. Putti serves May wine to the guests.

Sirius barks at Kaltenberg, who says: "That beast is even more savage than Alfred Kerr."

Rahel looks enchanting. She is wearing a cocktail dress made from midnight-blue silk.

Andreas Cohn stands there reverently at the edge of the circle.

"I hear from my daughter that you like to play the violin," says Father Liliencron.

"Yes," he replies.

"The violin," says Liliencron, miming a fiddling movement. "Is there still any future in that?"

"Yes," answers Cohn.

"Interesting," murmurs Liliencron. "I thought the jazz trumpet was the instrument of tomorrow."

"Tomorrow," says Cohn. "Who knows if we'll even live to see it."

"You think we might not?"

Cohn is about to give an answer that will offer an insight into his pessimistic worldview. But then Else approaches with a glass of May wine in her hand. She is already a little tipsy.

"What are you two talking about? Hopefully nothing too serious?"

"No, no," Liliencron assures her. "We're just chatting about the future."

Else takes Andreas by the hand and leads him over to Putti.

"Putti!" she calls. "Here's one of your countrymen."

"*Grüezi*," says Putti courteously.

The two Swiss expatriates exchange a few words in their native language, which makes them sound like ventriloquists who have come down with a cold.

Georg seeks out Andreas. "Else tells me you're worried about us."

Andreas nods. "Yes. I see dark times ahead for German Jews if things go on like this. And things *will* go on like this."

Professor Weidenfels comes over. "I hear," he says to Andreas, "that you have a famous name."

"Well, I still have to live up to it," says Andreas, exercising his modesty.

Weidenfels turns to Georg: "His father, Marcus Cohn, is the last white knight. I know many Jewish emigrants who owe their lives to him."

Liliencron joins in the conversation. "There it is again, that word. *Emigration*. Are you another one of these Zionists, Herr Cohn?"

Andreas replies: "My grandfather founded Zionism, together with Theodor Herzl."

Liliencron answers: "But we won't let anyone drive us away. That's exactly what Hitler wants. We're Germans. We belong in Germany."

He walks off dramatically.

"You see, Andreas, that's what I mean," says Georg. "To my father, Germany is still the country that gave him the golden Cothenius Medal. The home of Goethe. Of Beethoven's symphonies."

Liliencron clinks his glass with the cocktail stirrer. "Dear guests," he calls, "our friend Hans Fallada will now read a chapter from his new novel *Iron Gustav* for our entertainment."

*

Autumn has arrived. A thick blanket of cloud lies over the city, and it will soon shrug off the first snow.

The atmosphere in the Liliencron house is heavyhearted. As if there were a premonition of imminent developments which will spell doom for the family.

Sirius has already picked up the scent.

The routes for his walks are still the same, but many familiar faces have disappeared. The cobbler Horowitz, who always chatted nicely with him, is no longer there. The Finkelstein coffee roasting house, where it used to smell so wonderful, has closed down.

Other old acquaintances seem distracted or nervous. Herr Hoffmann, for example, who used to consider some good playacting worth a nut triangle. Or two.

Sirius sits down in front of the café and wags his tail expectantly.

Herr Hoffmann raises his head only briefly. "You again? What do you want now?"

Sirius jumps into the air on all fours.

"Yes, yes," murmurs Hoffmann absentmindedly. "Very nice."

No nut triangle.

Part of Sirius's repertoire is the number where he trots along on two legs and stretches his right paw out in a Hitler salute. He knows from experience that it goes down particularly well with humans in brown uniform. They return the greeting cheerfully and make quips like: "It looks like our party has made quite an impression on the dog."

But even that has changed now. A policeman stops Sirius and shouts at him: "Are you making fun of our Führer, you filthy mongrel?"

The reprimand is accompanied by a kick.

Everything is very strange. What's going on? Georg must have been right when he said: "This is no longer our country."

Sirius is contemplative as he sets off on his way home. He makes a quick detour to make sure his tree is still there.

The tree is still there.

*

The postman has no idea that today he is delivering a letter which will change the fate of the Liliencron family forever. Putti is on holiday, so the professor receives the letter himself.

The delivery is from the Leopoldina. The envelope is embossed with the words "German National Academy of Sciences."

Mail from the Leopoldina is a rare occurrence. Liliencron opens the letter on the spot.

We are writing to inform you that non-Aryan academics are to be excluded from membership with immediate effect. Your teaching contract has been suspended. Salary and pension entitlements have also ceased.

With regards, Professor Dr. Emil Abderhalden, President of the German National Academy of Sciences.

Liliencron tucks the letter into the inside pocket of his suit jacket and pulls on his overcoat. He takes the dog collar and lead from the coat rack, which immediately prompts Sirius to rush over joyfully. Together, they set off to the Neuer See in the Tiergarten. They sit down on a park bench by the water.

The lake was immortalized thirty years ago in one of Lovis Corinth's most beautiful paintings, on a gloomy day like today. Liliencron often comes here when he needs peace to think.

"I don't know what to do anymore, Sirius," he says.

Sirius nestles up close to him.

"My existence. Do you understand? That *was* my existence."

Sirius senses that his friend is in despair. Dogs can sense these things. They know what despair is, albeit generally in relation to more trivial causes.

Liliencron is angry with himself. Was he blind?

On Opernplatz, a mob burned books by Heinrich Heine while singing the Horst Wessel song. "Everything non-German into the flames!" they roared.

Professor Heisig has been dismissed, as has Professor Bernstein. Fritz Mahler has emigrated. Georg is being subjected to constant beatings. Germany has become a barbaric land.

"All of it really happened, I know that! Why didn't I want to acknowledge it? I was too proud. I convinced myself that the bearer of the golden Cothenius Medal didn't need to be afraid of these barbarians.

"But now I am afraid," he admits quietly. "What will become of us?"

Liliencron buries his face in his hands.

Sirius feels drops of rain on his fur. He looks up and realizes they are tears.

A man crying in despair is the saddest sight in the world.

Liliencron tries to pull himself together.

"Georg wanted to become a doctor," he says. "But Sauerbruch isn't even in contact with us anymore."

He sobs.

"And Else. She has talent. She could be a wonderful pianist, don't you think?"

Sirius nods.

"Where do we go from here?"

At moments like these, Sirius regrets the fact that he is not really a conversation partner. He just doesn't have the words.

"Humans have been around for 160,000 years," murmurs Liliencron. "And yet it only took Hitler five to destroy humanity."

A duck swimming sedately on the lake is unimpressed. Ducks have been around for roughly 30 million years.

"I hate myself," says Liliencron. "I'm ashamed of myself."

*

The night follows. Sirius is torn abruptly from his sleep. He hears voices, sees flames. Is he dreaming?

Sirius jumps up onto the windowsill. Fire! Ghostly clouds of smoke sweep over the rooftops, glowing fiercely. The coal-black billowing mass spits out blazing sparks—the synagogue on Fasanenstrasse has gone up in flames.

Vehicles hurtle past, men march up. They're wearing boots, hats and red armbands. Sirius hopes they are the firemen. But the men are jeering. One lights up a cigarette in a leisurely fashion.

A man in a hat, who actually looks very respectable, is working the crowd up into a frenzy: "Down with the Jews!" The cry is echoed from all throats, more and more violently, increasingly wild. On command, the tailgate of a truck opens, and iron bars roll down onto the street like claps of thunder. The men grab the bars and storm off. They smash the windows of Jewish shops, one after the other. The glass panes shatter, splinters flash through the air, layer upon layer of shards cover the ground. The sound is deafening.

Finally, the police arrive. But they don't intervene. Quite the opposite, in fact. A policeman pulls out his pistol and shoots into an upper-floor window, where a light can be seen burning. This incites the mob even more. The men break down the front doors to the buildings and force their way into the apartments, shouting, "Down with the Jews!"

Families are driven out onto the streets in their night-gowns. Sirius recognizes Albert Salomon. He is the Liliencron family's doctor. Trembling, he holds his wife and children by the hands. In front of an armband-wearing youth, who is already swinging his cudgel, he throws himself to his knees and pleads for his life. The boy spits on his head.

Sirius longs to jump at the youth's throat. He growls and bares his teeth. But he can't do anything against the pack out there alone. He has to warn his family.

The Liliencrons' bedrooms are on the peaceful, rear-side of the house. Sirius jumps up against the doors and barks.

Georg is the first to appear. "What's wrong? It's the middle of the night!"

Still half asleep, he follows the dog over to the window. Then he looks down at the street and freezes in shock.

By now, the mob has grown to several hundred men. The ones with the armbands have been joined by passersby and voyeurs. They have grabbed everything from inside the shops and thrown it onto the pavement. A troop stands there at the ready, covering the loot with gasoline and setting it on fire. Others force their way into apartments to plunder them. The street looks as though it is made of glass, so high are the mountains of shards. "Down with the Jews!" roars the mob.

Only now does Georg realize that the thick clouds of smoke are not coming from the flames on the street. He sees the immense wall of fire where the synagogue used to be.

Else comes over, rubbing her eyes. "Has something happened?"

Georg replies: "Yes, now it really has."

The firemen take great care to ensure that the water hoses don't extinguish the flames of the synagogue, but instead prevent the blaze from spreading to non-Jewish buildings.

Else screams: "No!" She is thinking of Andreas. Is he being driven out of his house at this very moment by men with bludgeons?

As her parents approach the window, Else breaks down and faints.

Naturally, the first thing Liliencron notices is the smallest detail amid the chaos. "There's Zinke. Caretaker Zinke."

He watches as Zinke distributes canisters of gasoline.

Then he broadens his viewpoint and takes in the whole inferno. Shard by shard. He is rooted to the spot. Lost for words.

He puts his arm around Georg. Then he turns away and tends to Else.

Rahel has covered her face with her hands. "Where are the police? Why is no one calling the police?"

"The police are there already," says Georg. "They're protecting the criminals."

One apartment after the other is emptied. The henchmen's boots thunder through every stairwell. "Are there Jews living here?"

"Yes, upstairs," the neighbors denounce.

Rahel sees families streaming out of the houses. The police separate them, seize the fathers and take them into custody. Protective custody, they are calling it.

The mothers hold their youngest children in their arms and the eldest by the hand. Some of them had time to grab blankets as they left. Most stand there shivering in the cold. It's November.

Then, suddenly, the horror is at close proximity. Fists hammer against the Liliencrons' front door.

"Oh God," cries Rahel.

"It's time to get out of here!" shouts Georg.

Crowbars smash the lock. An ax splinters into the wood. "Down with the Jews!"

"Where can we go?" whispers Liliencron.

"To Uncle Benno's!" hisses Georg.

They can already hear voices in the hallway as they run through the conservatory into the open air, jump over the hedge and seek shelter in the house next door.

*

For the first time in his life, Benno Fritsche, the great actor, is confronted with a dramatic situation without being appropriately prepared in terms of costume and lighting.

He comes straight out of bed, standing before the Liliencrons in his underpants and vest. His hair looks like cauliflower.

"What's got into you?" he asks, dumbfounded.

Liliencron tries to give a condensed summary of the events. Rahel sobs.

Georg and Else stare into the distance.

"So, in a nutshell," says Benno, "we all need a cognac."

No one disagrees. Benno pours.

"Those arseholes!" he cries.

"It's my own fault," says Liliencron. "I shouldn't have stuck my head in the sand for so long."

Rahel strokes his hand.

"Having your head in the sand," quipped Benno, "is still better than having sand in your head."

"The synagogue is on fire!" says Georg.

"Terrible, absolutely terrible," responds Benno. "But right now let's focus on the future. Your lives are at stake."

He excuses himself, freshens up and reappears in evening dress.

"Where's Levi, by the way?"

"Sirius!" cries Else.

"Of course," says Benno, "that's who I meant."

Liliencron jumps up. "Where's Sirius?"

Rahel: "Why, isn't he here?"

"Sirius!" cries Georg.

* * *

It seems that Sirius has stayed behind to guard the house.

"We forgot him," says Else, breaking down into tears.

At that moment, the doorbell rings. They hear voices. A fist beats against the door.

Benno gets up, straightens his dress shirt and cummerbund and strides to the entrance. He opens the door.

"*Geheime Staatspolizei*," says a voice.

Benno Fritsche bows.

"Are there Jews living here?" barks the policeman gruffly.

"Jews?" asks Fritsche in amazement. "What on earth gives you that idea?"

"There are Jews living next door," responds the policeman.

"Well, there aren't any here."

The policeman looks him up and down. "Are you sure about that?"

Fritsche, condescendingly: "You clearly don't know who I am!"

"Who are you, then?" asks the policeman.

Fritsche strikes a pose: "Benno Fritsche. Actor. Film star. Party member."

The policeman, meekly now: "Please accept my apologies."

The door closes.

Benno returns to the living room with a beaming smile: "So? How was I?"

The Liliencrons are trembling on the living room chairs, as pale as corpses.

One of them is missing: Georg.

"Where's Georg?" asks Benno.

"He went back to the house," says Liliencron. "To look for Sirius."

*

Sirius is sitting by the window. He looks out at the hell on earth and thinks: "Are those really humans?"

He looks up into the night sky. The light in the darkness, his comrade in arms, is nowhere to be seen. Has the star given up hope? Or is it just that the swathes of smoke are limiting the universe to right above the rooftops?

Sirius hears the boots, the voices, the gunshots.

He thinks back to when he was a little dog. Back to when he crawled into the farthest corner, rolled himself up into a lifeless ball and pretended he was an old cushion.

But now he is a big dog.

The men push open the door to the parlor and look around.

"Where are those Jewish vermin?" bellows one.

"Vermin!" roars the other, an ax in his hand.

Their gaze falls on Sirius.

Sirius fearlessly trots over to the two men, stops right in front of them, sits up and raises his right paw in a Hitler salute.

The men are astonished.

"Well, would you look at that!" says one.

The other one is speechless. He even lets the ax drop in shock.

* * *

They came to exterminate some Jews, but instead find themselves being greeted by a dog with the Hitler salute.

Their blind hate has suddenly evaporated. They even feel slightly fatigued. Exhaustion from all the barbarism.

"Do you reckon there's anything to drink here?" asks one.

They search the kitchen, open the fridge and come back with two beers.

"*Prost!*" they toast, sinking back onto the couch with a sigh. They are struggling to keep their eyes open.

"That was good, but tiring," says one.

A while later, they stand up again, stretch and roam through the house. When they get to the library, they grab books at random.

"*Plankton,*" says one with contempt.

"Look," says the other. "*Mein Kampf!*"

Baffled, he holds the book up in the air.

Sirius hurries over, sits up and begs, then flings his right paw upward. The men grin.

"Well, I think it's pretty obvious," says one. "There are no Jews living here."

The other nods and retrieves his ax from the floor.

They are just about to leave the house when they hear a cry.

"Sirius!"

The dog pricks up his ears, turns and dashes off.

The men immediately follow him into the garden. They can just about make out the silhouette of a figure in the darkness.

"*Halt!* Stay where you are!" shouts one.

"Hands up!" orders the other, pulling out his pistol.

The figure comes toward them with his hands held high.

"Who are you?" asks one.

"Name and address!" bellows the other.

"Georg Liliencron," answers the figure. "I live here."

The men pull him into the living room.

"Liliencron," says one. "Nice name."

"Nice name," repeats the other, slamming his fist into Georg's face.

"Nice house," says one.

"Nice Jew house," says the other. "That mutt pulled a fast one on us."

He picks up the ax and demolishes the couch that the two of them were sitting on just minutes ago. Their energy has returned.

"You're coming with us," says one.

"Protective custody," says the other. "We'll make sure nothing happens to you."

Georg lets them lead him away without a word. He's shaking with rage. And trembling with fear.

That very night, Georg ends up at the collection point in Levetzowstrasse. He is one of thousands who will be forced to walk barefoot to the Putlitzbrücke the next day. At Moabit train station, the freight trains are already standing at the ready. Final destination: Sachsenhausen concentration camp.

Protective custody.

*

The next morning, the sun rises at 7:42 A.M. Liliencron knows this because he is staring relentlessly at his watch.

Eight in the morning will be the earliest he can reach Emil Abderhalden, the president of the Leopoldina. As the discoverer of Abderhalden's enzymes and an advocate of eugenics, he has a good relationship with the Reich Ministry.

Uncle Benno has put on some fresh coffee. For Rahel and Else. He and Liliencron stick to the cognac. Sirius is slumbering. Last night is still haunting him.

"My home is your home," says Uncle Benno. "You're safe here for now."

Good old Fritsche. He's putting his own life at risk. The coffee could cost him his career. Snoops and squealers are working overtime today.

8 A.M. comes at last.

"Abderhalden," says the voice on the other end of the line.

Liliencron wishes him a good morning.

"My dear Liliencron," says Abderhalden. "I'm so sorry about the dismissal notice. But unfortunately there was no other way."

Liliencron interrupts him. He recounts the events of the previous night. He reports that Georg has disappeared without a trace. And closes with the words: "You've taken my honor from me, and I have to live with that. But I beg you from the bottom of my heart: Don't take my son too. That I cannot live with."

Abderhalden is embarrassed. "I understand, my dear man, but I have nothing to do with that."

"Put in a good word for him," pleads Liliencron. "You know people in high places."

"I know," responds Abderhalden. "But I can't exactly ring Rosenberg or Goebbels about—if you'll excuse me saying this—some family matter."

He hangs up.

Liliencron is distraught: "Is there no one who can help?"

He goes through a list of his social circle in his mind. Other Jews are in need of help themselves right now. And the non-Jews won't do a damn thing.

Besides, what Jew could call Goebbels anyway?

"Lorre!" cries Rahel.

"Lorre?" asks Liliencron, startled. A name from long-gone times when Rahel was dating a young actor named László Löwenstein, who later renamed himself Peter Lorre. A few years ago, Lorre emigrated to Hollywood.

"Goebbels himself advised him to leave the country!" emphasizes Rahel.

Liliencron shakes his head. "Why would Peter Lorre help us?"

"We were in love," says Rahel. "Very much in love."

What husband likes to hear that? If there's one thing that Liliencron could do without right now, then it's another stab to the heart.

Absurd; here the Liliencrons sit, in Berlin, in the darkest hour of their lives—and their hope lies in Hollywood!

Lorre!

But does anyone even have his telephone number?

Benno Fritsche, still in evening attire, but with his shirt open and a great deal of cognac inside him, strides over to the desk and proudly fetches his address book.

"Here's his number."

He beams from ear to ear. "We shot a movie together once. *M—A City Hunts a Murderer.* I was still relatively unknown back then. It was my first speaking role."

"*A City Hunts a Murderer,*" murmurs Liliencron. "Now it would be called: *A City Becomes a Murderer.*"

Where can Georg be? Every one of them is still picturing themselves standing before that window. Else sees the men with the iron bars. Liliencron sees the policeman nonchalantly smoking a cigarette. Sirius can't forget the youth in front of whom Albert Salomon fell to his knees.

Is Georg in the hands of these monsters? It is a terrible, unbearable thought.

Lorre!

"I'll call him," says Rahel.

She dictates a series of numbers to the woman at the telephone exchange. "It's a long-distance call," she says, with a self-important air.

The line rustles, crackles, rattles—then, all of a sudden, an unfamiliar, crystal clear ringtone can be heard at the other end.

"Hello?" says a voice.

"Peter?" asks Rahel hesitantly. It's him. The last time Rahel spoke with him was ten years ago, only very briefly, on the sidelines of a film premiere. He always used to call her "Sausage." "Sausage!" he cries again now.

Rahel immediately tells him about the severity of the situation. The hell in Berlin. Georg.

Else imagines every single word racing along an unimaginably long cable which lies in the depths of the ocean, eyed warily by huge fish, before emerging again in front of the coast of America, spanning the entire continent, and eventually ending up in that very telephone receiver.

A miracle.

But can the cable perform miracles too?

If so, then this is the decisive moment. Their last hope.

Lorre listens. He keeps saying, "How awful," again and again. "How awful."

"Help us!" pleads Rahel. "Can you help us?"

"I'll try," says Lorre. "I promise."

Then he adds: "Don't waste any time getting out of there. You need to leave Berlin at once. Come to Hollywood!"

Hollywood!

Rahel closes her eyes. "What's wrong with you?" asks a voice. It's Clark Gable.

"Nothing," answers Rahel in her dream. "I'm just a bit tired."

"May I introduce my friend Humphrey Bogart?" says Gable.

"Only if I can dance with him!" says Rahel.

"It would be my pleasure," Bogart says with a smile.

They dance a mambo. More wildly than Rahel has ever danced in her life.

Peter Lorre winks at her.

"What's wrong with you?" asks Liliencron. "I thought you fainted."

"No, I was just dreaming a little," replies Rahel.

Sirius barks.

Someone is rattling the garden gate.

Benno Fritsche steps out onto the terrace. He sees a young man in the neighboring garden and challenges him: "What do you want?"

"I'm looking for the Liliencron family," says the man.

When Sirius wags his tail, the stranger begins to make a better impression on Fritsche.

"Andreas!" cried Else, running into the arms of her beloved.

"You're mad!" she says. "Going out on the streets like this? You're putting your life in danger!"

"I have important news for you," says Andreas. "For all of us."

"Andreas Cohn," he says to Fritsche, introducing himself.

"Benno Fritsche," says Fritsche.

"Of course. I recognize you from the movies," Andreas replies. With those words, he instantly wins Fritsche's affections.

"Pack your things!" cries Andreas. "It's time to go."

Liliencron stares at him in disbelief. "Where?"

Andreas: "To America!" He explains: "My father has already prepared all of the papers. Tonight we go to Basel. After that, I'll accompany you to Genoa, and you'll travel on by ship to America."

"I'm afraid that just won't be possible," says Liliencron. "Georg needs to be back with us first."

"Georg?" asks Andreas in horror. "Where's Georg?"

"We don't know," says Liliencron flatly. "We just hope he's still alive."

*

Willy Kaminski is stunned by the crowd of people gathering in front of his bakery on Erasmusstrasse. He makes good bread, granted, but not so good as to explain this. The pavement is filling rapidly. What's going on?

The people want to watch the Jews passing by.

The march of the "protective custody internees" begins at the collection point in Levetzowstrasse and leads up to the Putlitzbrücke, where the freight trains are waiting to take them to Sachsenhausen concentration camp.

As the procession passes the bakery, Willy Kaminski runs out to stand before the death squadron.

"You should be ashamed of yourselves!" he shouts. "Shame on Hitler!"

His corpse is found a short while later. Executed in sight of the gawking onlookers, who stand by the side of the road and pelt the Jews with stones.

*   *   *

Moabit freight train station. At Platform No. 69, the carriages stand ready.

The police separate the convoy into groups of a hundred men, directing each toward a wagon. An SS Obersturmführer is overseeing the proceedings.

Georg is still managing to walk upright. But he has lost almost all his strength. Others are crawling with exhaustion and have to be kicked up the platform, the older men in particular.

A rabbi walking with a stick is beaten into a wagon with the butt of a rifle.

"*Caracho, caracho!*" call the SS men. Everything has to be done quickly; they want to get back home to their families in time for dinner.

Toward midday, the train sets off.

The wagon in which Georg is imprisoned is normally used for transporting cattle. It has grills. Georg watches the north of the city rushing past him. Reinickendorf. Frohnau. Waidmannslust.

A completely normal day in Berlin.

The rabbi sings a Yiddish song softly to himself. "*S'brent. Undzer Shtetl brent.*"

> "*Don't stand there, brothers, looking on,*
> *not lifting a hand,*
> *Don't stand there, brothers, douse the fire,*
> *Our little town is burning.*"

Georg thinks of caretaker Zinke, who handed out the gasoline canisters used to set the city on fire.

Suddenly, the train comes to an abrupt halt.

Birkenwerder station.

A big black limousine is waiting by the platform. A chauffeur is standing next to it, his hand raised in a Hitler salute.

An SS man jumps out of the train and goes over to him. They speak to each other briefly, then the SS man comes back.

Minutes pass by.

Then the SS man steps back out onto the platform again. He has a loudspeaker with him.

"Attention, announcement!" he bellows into the loudspeaker. "Prisoner Georg Liliencron! Please make yourself known immediately!"

Georg cannot believe his ears.

He rattles at the bars. "Here! Here!"

The sliding door of the wagon opens. The SS man orders: "Come with me!"

The chauffeur salutes as Georg approaches and takes a seat in the back of the limousine.

"Personal chauffeur of Reich Minister Dr. Joseph Goebbels," says the man by way of introduction. "Where would you like to go?"

"Home," says Georg.

*

It is just before midnight. The Liliencrons go into their house, for the first time since the inferno, for the last time before their journey into the unknown.

The two empty beer bottles still stand on the glass table. It is a sight even more monstrous than that of the destroyed settee.

Liliencron goes and stands in front of his bookshelves. He wants to take a book with him as a memento, but which one? He chooses Heinrich Hoffmann's *Struwwelpeter*. This was the book he learned to read with.

He sinks absentmindedly down into the armchair, next to the two empty beer glasses, and leafs through *Struwwelpeter*.

"Carl!" cries Rahel. "Have you lost your mind?"

"No, no," murmurs Liliencron. "I'm just nostalgic. But perhaps that is a kind of insanity."

He puts the book back on the shelf and chooses instead, pragmatically, his own work *Phytoplankton and Photosynthesis*. After all, you never know when it might come in useful to be able to prove yourself as a plankton expert.

He leaves the golden Cothenius Medal hanging on the wall.

Rahel stands in front of her wardrobe, wishing she could take everything. The pink outfit would be ideal for cocktail parties. And the blue evening gown is an absolute dream.

Don't be foolish, she determines: a new start is a new start. She packs her jewelry. And a few framed photographs.

Else packs only sheet music into her suitcase. Felix Mendelssohn Bartholdy's Violin Concerto, op. 64. Her love story.

Georg takes nothing. Nothing at all. And yet his baggage weighs the most.

In the end, just *one* suitcase stands by the door. One small suitcase. The past must be condensed if it wants to make it to the future.

Sirius senses that this is a farewell to yesterday. Perhaps forever. He slinks out of the house and runs off to the tree, *his* tree.

How does a dog say good-bye to a tree? He doesn't know.

Sirius is sure he sees the tree bowing down softly. But perhaps it was just the wind.

Liliencron fetches the car from the garage.

The green Mercedes swallows up Carl, Rahel, Georg, Else, Andreas and Sirius. Just like the suitcase swallowed up their past.

*

The meeting place is a barn in Hohentengen, a village on the Rhine not far from the Swiss border. At three o' clock on the dot.

"A man called Ernest Prodolliet will be expecting you." Andreas has in front of him the notes from the telephone conversation he had with his father yesterday.

Sure enough, the barn door opens punctually to the very minute, and a silver Bentley comes driving out. A man in a suit and tie climbs out.

Ernest Prodolliet is Chancellor of the Swiss Consulate Agency in Bregenz. He asks the Liliencrons for their papers, then stamps every one of the documents without a word.

"I'm afraid you'll have to leave the car here," he says. "Please put it in the barn."

He closes the barn door again and motions for them to get into his car.

No one can beat Herr Prodolliet when it comes to radiating calm and authority. He drives toward the border.

The German border officials salute.

Herr Prodolliet shows his diplomat pass and says: "The ladies and gentlemen have the appropriate papers."

An officer inspects them, nods and opens the barrier.

"Is that the Rhine, the one you told me about?" asks Else as they drive over the bridge.

"Yes, that's the Rhine," responds Andreas. "Welcome to freedom!"

There's not a dry eye in the car, apart from those belonging to Herr Prodolliet, of course.

Dinner in Lucerne.

The waitress suggests "*G'schnätzlets* with *Röschti*."

"We'd best not," replies Liliencron. "That sounds too aggressive. I'd prefer something more peaceful. Soup, for example."

Herr Prodolliet takes care of the bill. He knows that Jews are not permitted to take more than ten Reichsmarks with them when leaving the country. Their entire fortune is forfeited to the state. He knows because he stamped this document too.

This place smells different from Berlin somehow, thinks Sirius. He can't define exactly what it is, but it must have something to do with the fresh manure on the fields.

Their journey leads them over the Alps toward Italy. In the early-morning light, they reach Genoa.

The *Conte di Savoia* is already docked in the harbor. The ship is an imposing sight. It measures a thousand feet in length, can take 2,200 passengers and is one of the biggest ocean liners in the world. The two mighty funnels are already steaming for the long journey to New York.

The area around the terminal is heaving with people. Passengers, chauffeurs, porters, sailors, photographers, policemen, musicians, pickpockets, ice-cream sellers, souvenir hawkers. And, of course, all the onlookers who want to witness the behemoth setting sail.

"Take care of yourself," whispers Else. "Promise me that we'll see each other again!"

Andreas gives her a kiss which says: Yes, I promise.

The Liliencrons are now crossing the last bridge. Into the belly of the *Conte di Savoia*, where they find themselves in a majestic hall of marble columns. By chance, they spot Ludwig Mies van der Rohe among the crowd; he has also left Berlin. A steward accompanies the passengers to their cabins.

The captain sounds the ship's horn three times and fires up the engines. They're off.

The Liliencron family goes over to the ship's rail. A mighty gorge of sea spray gapes open behind the stern.

The crowd of people cheer and wave. One of them is Andreas, their savior. And Herr Prodolliet, of course.

Sirius deliberates. The smell he liked best of their journey so far was in Lucerne.

If everything goes on like this, then it will be fine.

PART 2

WHILE BERLIN STILL lies buried under snow, in Hollywood the magnolias are already blooming and the air is fragrant with jasmine. The Pacific mixes a pinch of salt into the air, but this is only perceptible for those who live high up in Beverly Hills, like John Clark.

John Clark is the "next Gary Cooper," people say. He has the kind of looks any man would love to have, and women have gone crazy for him ever since he was just a lifeguard in the Garden of Allah hotel.

He was discovered by Jack Warner himself.

"Do you have to be in water?" Warner asked him from the edge of the swimming pool. "Or could you imagine doing something on dry land?"

You would need to shift completely into the mind-set of a lifeguard in order to understand that, at that moment, he really had no idea what the world outside the swimming pool had to offer.

He stared at the business card which the older man pressed into his hand: Jack Warner, Warner Bros. Film Studios, Hollywood.

The following day, John Clark's career began.

A few years have passed since then, and by now one can safely say that John Clark has done pretty well on dry land. He has conquered Hollywood, he is a star. But above all, it's his nocturnal activities with which he's really made a name for himself.

"When does John Clark sleep?" read a recent headline in the *Hollywood Reporter*.

Hedda Hopper, the *Reporter*'s famous gossip columnist, is hot on his heels. She follows while he, Humphrey Bogart and a few friends throw so many martinis down their throats in the Formosa that they exhaust even the bartender. Then they're off to the Trocadero, where a volcano called John Clark erupts on the dance floor. At dawn, the Polo Lounge is opened especially for him, because he has a craving for caviar. The blonde with whom he eventually disappears into his suite doesn't, however. She has a hankering for vodka instead, which results in the guests in the neighboring room complaining about the "sound of furniture shattering." Nonetheless, just a short while later John Clark appears in the studio, fresh and cheerful—filming can begin. He is in top form. That's how the story goes, night after night, day after day.

And yet John Clark is married. He has a wife and kids. And not just any wife, but Gloria Hayson. She was a Hollywood star herself, but she sacrificed her career for a family life and is now growing increasingly lonely in their palace.

Hedda Hopper is already dropping hints that Gloria is an alcoholic, and a suicidal one at that. A scandal is looming.

Jack Warner summons John Clark into his office.

"I made you," he says wistfully.

The words sound as though God is speaking to one of his creatures, moved by the memory of the day when it learned to walk upright and became a human being.

And that's exactly how it is. In Hollywood, Jack Warner is God.

"I fished you out of the water," he continued. "And I can throw you back in anytime. Don't forget that."

John Clark nods reverently. For a while, they sit there silently across from each other, the white-haired film mogul and the man he plucked from obscurity.

"Little fish," murmurs the mogul. "What was your name again?"

"Giovanni Clarizzo," answers the little fish.

He had emigrated from Sicily only a few months before he became a lifeguard in the Garden of Allah hotel.

"I gave you the name John Clark," says the mogul. "Live up to it."

Another long silence.

The secretary enters the room and points at the clock. The next appointment is waiting.

Jack Warner is already on his way to the door when he says, seemingly as a casual aside: "Go back to your family, John."

John wants to say something in response, but he can't get the words out.

"What you need now is some peace and quiet," Warner says, smiling. "That's all you need. Herr Liliencron will take care of it."

John hesitates. "Herr Liliencron?"

"A friend of some friends," replies Warner. "I helped with his entry papers. Now he needs a job. You are his job. He will be your new chauffeur, your guardian angel." He spreads his arms out wide. "Make him feel welcome in Hollywood! He's from Berlin. Doesn't speak a word of English, so he's very tight-lipped. Doesn't know a soul, so he's discreet. He won't even notice that the young woman fooling around on the backseat with you is Rita Hayworth."

Warner lays his fingers on his lips as a sign of discretion.

*

Carl Liliencron is sitting for the first time in the brand-new silver Chevrolet the studio has provided for the guardian angel. On this beautiful morning, he is driving down Sunset Boulevard. The tall palm trees which line the street stretch themselves out toward the sun. Now it's finally clear where the sun is when it's absent in Berlin—in Hollywood. And it isn't just making a guest appearance in the sky, but is under permanent contract, a dependable spotlight which consistently provides the same fairy-tale light.

No wonder, really, that Jack Warner picked this corner of the earth for his dream factory.

Liliencron turns into Rexford Drive. He still needs to use

PART 2

a street map to orientate himself. Laurel Way should be
somewhere around here.

The magnificent villas are concealed behind immense
hedges from which hosts of gardeners hang, trying to give
the foliage as quadratic a form as possible. That's how it has
to be.

John Clark lives in a palace. It effortlessly outshines even
the ones which were erected along the banks of the Loire in
the Renaissance.

The gate opens as though by an invisible hand, and Liliencron
glides up the driveway in the Chevrolet, wide-eyed in won-
derment. A servant in a tailcoat is already awaiting him.

And that's just the overture. The actual opera begins
after the walk through the hall out onto the terrace, where
the eye sweeps across a landscape reminiscent of the Scottish
Highlands: lakes on which little ships pitch and toss,
meadows with ponies galloping around, pavilions, foun-
tains, even a fairground carousel for the children.

Liliencron can't believe his eyes. Has he, without noticing
it, shuffled off his mortal coil, and this is paradise? Is he in
the curvature of space-time that Einstein always speaks
about?

He looks for signs of human life. Then John Clark comes
toward him. Completely unsuspecting that he has just
become associated with the theory of relativity.

"Welcome to Hollywood!" says John Clark, shaking his
hand.

"Thank you!" says Liliencron.

* * *

John Clark explains cheerfully to his visitor how he recently acquired the adjoining piece of land from James Stewart, for the sole purpose of tearing down his house and erecting a chimpanzee enclosure in its place.

"My name is Carl Liliencron," replies Liliencron.

Clark pauses. Then he remembers Jack Warner telling him that the man was from Berlin, that he doesn't speak a word of English and that he doesn't even know who Rita Hayworth is.

"Rita Hayworth?" asks Clark, just to make sure.

Liliencron shakes his head in confusion.

So Warner wasn't exaggerating, for a change.

The oddball from Berlin looks like a civil servant, thinks Clark. If he'd had any say in it, his guardian angel would have looked quite different.

"Okay, let's go," decides John Clark.

He waves at his wife and the children, who are off in the distance feeding the flamingos.

"Family," he sighs, sinking into the backseat of the car.

"Yes," replies Liliencron.

"Do you have family?" asks Clark.

"Yes," replies Liliencron.

Other than that, their journey is a silent one.

"Warner Bros. Pictures" is spelled out in large letters over the entrance gate of the studio city. Gigantic billboards of current box office smashes are plastered over the facade. *Robin Hood* starring Errol Flynn, *Dark Victory* with Bette Davis, *Angels with Dirty Faces* with James Cagney and Humphrey Bogart.

The porter eyes the new silver Chevrolet warily. Only when he recognizes John Clark does he salute and open the barrier.

He instructs the chauffeur to hold the official studio badge up to the windshield.

"My name is Carl Liliencron," replies Liliencron.

It happens all of a sudden. The Chevrolet catches fire and blazes fiercely. Men with iron bars jump onto the hood and smash the windshield. Glass, nothing but glass everywhere. The caretaker, Zinke, is handing out the gasoline canisters. The porter roars: "Down with the Jews!"

Liliencron wrenches the steering wheel around and speeds into Klamtstrasse. Home! He has to save Sirius!

The Chevrolet skids across the studio grounds and comes to a standstill just seconds before colliding with the main building.

"Hey, man!" cries Clark. "What a drive!" He wipes the sweat from his brow. "That's Hitler style!"

Liliencron laughs hysterically. Then he falls unconscious.

John Clark isn't quite sure why, but he likes his new chauffeur.

*

Every Friday is payday. That's the norm in Hollywood. Even movie stars get paid on a weekly basis.

A chauffeur's salary is roughly equivalent to the amount the Clark family spends on flamingo feed each month.

When Carl puts the few bills down on the table each

payday, he always comments drily: "Hardly a noteworthy amount."

This new life in the new world often plunges him into existential-philosophical moods. What he once was, he is no more. So who is he? The nagging questions arise especially when he puts on his chauffeur's cap in the mornings. And in the evenings too, when he comes home. His existence has shrunk to the smallest of spaces: a bungalow, in which a suitcase stands. One of those wooden shacks that are being knocked up day after day in Hollywood so that even the minor employees can have a roof over their heads.

Carl stares into nothingness. The naked walls. The bare rooms. The silent days. The empty nights, nothing but black holes.

Only the suitcase is full of memories. When they awake, they haunt Liliencron. He is exhausted.

"What's the point of surviving if you're not living?"
"Oh, Carl," says Rahel. "We are living."
"My name is Carl Liliencron. That's all I can say."
Rahel takes her husband in her arms and comforts him.
"You can say 'yes' too. Try to say 'yes' more often."

In this respect, Sirius is having an easier time of it. He can communicate without any problems in the new homeland. He likes it in Hollywood.

He recently met a dog who works in the movie business. As an extra. It was a very interesting encounter. The dog told him that his dream is to work for Disney, as a dubbing voice for Goofy. But, as he knows very well, talent alone isn't enough—it's all about who you know.

Hollywood is a hard place. Sirius discovered that when his paws hurt after particularly long walks. There are hardly any paths with grass. It's all concrete.

He thinks back to Berlin. Is his tree still standing? Is the yellow ball still in the garden? In his haste, he forgot to take it with him. That rankles him at times.

Rahel is in the process of teaching him a new trick. Yowling chansons. "The French are very good at it," she says.

She puts a record on, and Sirius tries to yowl the melody. He does a pretty good job of it with Maurice Chevalier. The song "Y'a d'la joie" is about how the Eiffel Tower is bored.

If even the Eiffel Tower is bored, then how must Rahel feel? She's still looking for something to do with her time. The children have left home.

Georg has received a scholarship. His dream is coming true; he is studying medicine. He lives on the university campus in West Hollywood.

Else has taken on a post as a nanny in the house of Erich Wolfgang Korngold. The composer left Vienna five years ago and followed Max Reinhardt to Hollywood. Now he's contracted with Warner Bros., and in February he got his first Oscar for the film score to *Robin Hood*. Else is surrounded all day long by the sound of his piano playing.

Good old Jack Warner. He helps countless Jews to escape from Germany, he pulls strings in the White House, he takes the new arrivals under his wing and directs their journey from suffering to happiness, called destiny. He is a one-man dream factory.

Poor old Carl Liliencron. He is still having nightmares. In his heart, he's still the bearer of the golden Cothenius Medal. His eyes need to adjust, from plankton, which is tinier than ten thousandths of an inch, to Sunset Boulevard, which spans twenty-two miles. Hollywood is reaching for the stars, while Liliencron can't even fly yet.

But that will soon change. After all, he's a guardian angel now.

*

Peter Lorre celebrates his birthday with a party. The Liliencrons arrive at eight o'clock on the dot.

They are the first to arrive. And the only ones there. In Hollywood, people arrive late to prove how important they are. The later the hour, the more important. The rule applies to the unimportant people too. Someone who is unimportant comes later than someone who is even more unimportant.

A short man with a hat perched askew turns up relatively early. He seems to be familiar with the house and the garden, for he walks purposefully over to the barbecue and gets himself a bratwurst. Then he fetches a beer from the icebox.

"Billy Wilder," he says, introducing himself.

He claims to be one of Peter Lorre's closest friends. It wasn't so long ago that the two of them were sharing a room.

"One room!" emphasizes Wilder. "It was clear that at least one of us had to make it. Peter was the first, he became Mr. Moto. I wrote the screenplay for *Ninotchka* for Ernst Lubitsch, which wasn't bad, either. A Mexican cleaning woman has been living in the room ever since."

Liliencron laughs. For the first time since he stepped onto American soil, Rahel sees her husband roar with laughter.

"He's laughing!" she cries.

"That's my job," replies Wilder. "I sincerely hope your husband won't be the only one."

"It's wonderful to speak German again," says Liliencron.

"Is that your dog?" asks Wilder, pointing at Sirius, who is snuffling around the barbecue and wagging his tail. "What language does your dog speak?"

Liliencron is baffled. What language *does* Sirius speak?

"Look," says Wilder. "He wants a piece of sausage. He's wagging his tail. He wants to be happy. A sausage is a sausage, regardless of language. There's a universal language of happiness, you know."

The garden fills up. Erich von Stroheim, Vicki Baum, Otto Preminger, Marlene Dietrich, Robert Siodmak, Fritz Lang—everyone is there. Everyone who had to leave their homeland. Hollywood has suddenly become a neighborhood of Berlin.

Fanfare. Peter Lorre steps out onto the terrace. He greets his guests, and the small band plays "Lili Marleen." Everyone dances, and tears flow.

"It's my fault," calls Lorre, as he walks over to the Liliencrons.

He frames the word "fault" by gesticulating speech marks with his fingers, intended to illustrate his sarcasm.

"Stop!" calls Marlene Dietrich. "That was my invention."

"What?" interjects Fritz Lang. "Surely the only German hand motion that has a claim to copyright is the Hitler salute."

"My dear Liliencrons," says Peter Lorre, raising his glass. "You have to get out of Berlin! Come to Hollywood! That was my advice to you that day on the telephone. And now you're here."

Applause. Fanfare from the band. The guests embrace the Liliencrons and wish them luck.

Carl Liliencron has tears in his eyes.

"My God," says Rahel. "Now he's even crying."

"That's life," replies Robert Siodmak. "No happiness without tears. No sorrow without a smile."

The band plays "Why Have You Forgotten Waikiki?"

Billy Wilder is a force to be reckoned with on the dance floor. In Berlin, he occasionally had to make ends meet as a ballroom dance partner for widows.

"What's your dream?" he asks suddenly.

Liliencron shrugs. He doesn't understand the question.

Wilder clicks his fingers. "Singing? Then become a singer. Burgling? Then become a burglar. Reinvent yourself. You need a dream to get yourself up in the morning."

And with those words, he's already back on the dance floor.

* * *

At two in the morning, Humphrey Bogart sways up with his dog Zero on the lead. He's drunk.

"Who fancies a game of Skat?" he slurs. Lorre taught him the card game, and he's been addicted ever since.

Sirius and Zero sniff each other. It could be the beginning of a wonderful friendship.

The band plays "Over the Rainbow."

This is the night that Carl and Rahel Liliencron truly arrive in Hollywood. They dance, closely intertwined, even after the band has long stopped playing. Suddenly, they too are speaking the universal language of happiness.

"We're living," whispers Rahel.

"Yes," replies Carl.

*

One morning, Liliencron wakes up and decides that he will no longer be called Liliencron. For some reason, the name is standing in his way. Even though it's still unclear to him what that way is and where it might be leading. But the name is too cumbersome. It feels as though he has to constantly lug around the suitcase he emigrated here with.

"My name is Carl Liliencron."

He doesn't want to hear that sentence anymore. He doesn't want to be an outsider anymore. He wants to have the kind of name someone has when they belong.

Why not Carl Crown?

Short. Quick. Clear. Snazzy. Cheerful. Brilliant. Confident. Affluent.

That's it.

John Clark is the first to hear the new name, and he is very taken with it.

"Yeah," he says, "good idea. Makes things easier."

He looks the freshly baked Carl Crown up and down, then suggests: "New name, new clothes."

The two men have pretty much the same build, so the clothes the Hollywood star fetches from his wardrobe fit Carl perfectly.

A pair of white flannel trousers with colored pleats—fit.

A light-blue polo shirt and an ocher-colored silk sweater vest—fit.

A green double-breasted cashmere jacket—fits.

A pocket handkerchief: pink with a yellow diamond pattern.

Shoes: white full brogues with a Derby cut.

John Clark claps his hands with delight. "*Now* I like how my guardian angel looks!"

Carl Crown is still a little unsure. He looks like someone who wants to be a trumpet player in a jazz band.

But maybe that is what he wants, and he just doesn't know it yet.

"Let's go and have a drink!" says John Clark.

He says that a lot. Every time there's something to celebrate, in fact, and even if it's just some tiny insignificant detail, like a door opening after he rings the bell. Another reason to celebrate. John Clark was always in an excellent mood; you had to give him that.

* * *

They drive to the Formosa, sit up at the bar and order gin fizzes.

"Is Hitler really such a bad guy?" asks Clark.

"Yes," answers Crown.

"Do you play golf?" asks Clark.

"No," answers Crown.

Just the usual things people talk about at a bar. When they're really talking to each other for the first time.

"Do you like blondes?" asks Clark.

"Yes," answers Crown.

"And your girlfriend?"

"No girlfriend," says Crown.

"Is your wife a blonde?"

"No."

"No girlfriend?" John Clark throws his head back in laughter. "Well, that'll soon change with the way you look now."

Another round of gin fizzes. And another.

When Carl Crown comes home that night, his wife sees a drunken man in a light-blue polo shirt and an ocher-colored silk sweater vest.

Rahel cries bitterly.

In the early hours of the following morning, the German Wehrmacht marches into Poland. Adolf Hitler has sparked off the Second World War.

*

The year of 1939 will go down in movie history, everyone in Hollywood is already sure of that.

The Wizard of Oz is coming to movie theaters in August, *Stagecoach* in September, *Mr. Smith Goes to Washington* in October, *Ninotchka* in November, and finally, in December, *Gone With the Wind*.

The Great Dictator, *Rebecca* and *The Philadelphia Story* are currently being filmed.

One day, people will call this "The Golden Age," or something like that.

It's not a bad moment to be living in Hollywood. Carl Crown spends every free minute he has in the movie theater. He is learning the universal language of happiness. He has enough time, after all; his job as a guardian angel consists mainly of waiting around.

Every morning, at 6 A.M. on the dot, he picks up John Clark and chauffeurs him to the studio. Clark is filming *The Sea Hawk*, with Errol Flynn.

Crown then drinks a cup of coffee in the Brown Derby, before the matinee opens around the corner in the El Capitan Movie Palace.

At lunchtime, John Clark usually wants to do a "bit of exercise." By that, he means physical training with some starlet. He has his own bungalow on the studio grounds, of course, but too many curious reporters hang around there.

So his guardian angel drives the couple to a secluded clearing in Laurel Canyon and discreetly absents himself. The bottle of champagne on the backseat has to be cooled to just the right temperature. Based on his experience, after ten minutes it's usually safe for Crown to make his way back.

He then enjoys the afternoon program in one of the numerous cinemas on Hollywood Boulevard.

At six in the evening, the hardest part of his job begins. This is when John Clark is in the mood to party.

He asks to be driven straight to Don the Beachcomber, where a group of people are already waiting for him, ready to embark upon a martini marathon.

The later the hour, the harder things get for the guardian angel. In the Trocadero, he has to point demonstratively at his watch when a dancer lays her head in John Clark's lap. Charlie Dotter empties an ice bucket over his friend to cool him off.

"Time to go," says Crown.

"Aw, come on," pouts Clark, "let's just stop by the Banana House quickly."

The Banana House is not the kind of place to end the evening on a sedate note; to say that the venue has a lively atmosphere would be a major understatement.

A real-life grizzly bear lurches around on the dance floor in rhythm with the band, chimpanzees and impalas run around freely, pelicans fly through the air, the waiters sit on dromedaries, and the girls hang from vines. Both man and mammal dance the hula.

Carl Crown likes this place. There's absolutely nothing to remind him of Klamtstrasse here.

John Clark, of course, is quite keen to turn the night into a legendary one. But after just one drink, his guardian angel is already telling him it's time to go home.

At least Clark has a souvenir from the jungle with him.

A full-busted mamba, who nestles down lasciviously on the backseat.

Carl Crown recognizes the mamba. He saw her a few days ago in the film *Only Angels Have Wings*. Her name is Rita Hayworth.

*

Clearly John Clark is an animal lover, thinks Crown. So one day not long after, he takes Sirius with him to work.

"What's this then?" asks Clark in surprise. "The guardian angel brought reinforcements."

"This is Sirius," Crown explains. "I hope that's okay."

"No problem," replies Clark, "as long as he doesn't drop his needles. What do they call it with dogs?"

"Needles?" Crown doesn't understand.

"You know, like Christmas trees. We still have needles lying around the house from last Christmas. It was ten months ago. You can't get rid of the things."

"No, no, Sirius doesn't drop his needles," Crown assures him.

To err on the side of caution, Sirius keeps his distance, taking up residence on the front seat. Suddenly, the journey doesn't seem work-related anymore. More like a private whistle-stop tour of a man and his dog who just happen to have a Hollywood star on the backseat.

"You should go to the dog cemetery sometime," suggests Clark. "It's not far from here. Valentino's dog is buried there. Bogey's last dog too. It could be interesting for you, Sirius."

Sirius isn't so sure. But he acknowledges the gesture politely. He doesn't really want to think about death just yet. But if he did, then of course that would be the ideal place for it.

Life is much too short when you're a dog. Sirius broods. The lobster lives to 60 years old. The sturgeon to 150. The whale even lives to 200. It seems that living in water enables you to live longer. But what great experiences can you have underwater?

For example, how many sturgeons are currently being driven through Hollywood in a Chevrolet?

"Your dog is a little melancholic, don't you think?" asks Clark, as though he could read minds.

"Sometimes," replies Crown. "He gets it from me."

I know that guy, thinks Sirius, when they arrive at Warner Bros. and see Humphrey Bogart glowering down at them from the poster wall. Is his dog there too?

The porter bows knowingly and opens the barrier.

John Clark has a day off from filming today; he's meeting a young director named John Huston, who is planning to film Dashiell Hammett's *The Maltese Falcon*.

"It will be a film noir," enthuses Huston.

"Hopefully not too noir," says Clark. "Otherwise people won't be able to see me."

"I don't think you're right for the role," says Huston, abruptly ending their conversation.

* * *

"That was quick," remarks Crown in surprise.

"Ridiculous!" blusters Clark. "An amateur. He wants to shoot a movie in the dark. The man will never come to anything, you mark my words."

For the first time, John Clark is exhibiting the slightest trace of a bad mood.

"Let's go and have a drink," he suggests. It seems he even says it when there's nothing to celebrate.

They saunter over to the canteen.

Meanwhile, Sirius is exploring the studio grounds. Not the safest of places, he notes. Motorized trolleys hurtle toward him from all directions, crisscrossing past one another, carrying stagehands with props, cameramen with tripods, lighting technicians with spotlights—everything you can think of.

They beep as they weave their way through the narrow alleys between the halls, to make sure that no king, gangster, ghost or whatever else from any of the movies gets run over.

What's that red light blinking over the entrance of the biggest studio? Sirius is curious. He heads over to see what's going on.

A hall as immense as Berlin's Alexanderplatz has been decorated to represent the deck of a Spanish barque, currently engaged in a dramatic naval battle with the British fleet.

"Action!" yells the director. Hundreds of extras in period dress wave their swords around. A wind machine blasts into the sails.

Sirius is deeply impressed.

* * *

"Cut!" yells the director. "What's that mutt doing in there?"

Sirius ducks his head down.

"We're right in the middle of the decisive battle on the high seas and some mongrel wanders into the shot!" roars the director.

A marine officer puts Sirius back outside the door.

What a memorable debut.

For the first time ever, Sirius was on camera in Hollywood. And it won't be the last, either.

*

The whole family is gathered around the dinner table together for the first time in a long while. In Capri, a pizzeria on Melrose Avenue. Carl and Rahel live just around the corner, but their apartment is too small for everyone.

Germany is at war. France and England are supporting Poland. Russia is mobilizing.

"Just imagine!" says Carl.

Benno Fritsche has written to them. His new next-door neighbor is Karl-Heinrich Bodenschatz, a major general in the Ministry of Aviation.

"Not exactly the kind of neighbor you feel inclined to hop over the fence and see," wrote Benno.

"In our house," sighs Rahel.

"Do you remember how Uncle Benno outwitted that commander?" asks Else.

Georg thinks back to the freight train to Birkenwerder.

"Personal chauffeur of Reich Minister Dr. Goebbels. Where would you like to go?"

"To Hollywood, please!" cries Carl.

Rahel talks about the party at Peter Lorre's. "Humphrey Bogart is so handsome!"

Just the usual things people talk about when they've survived.

What was it Robert Siodmak said that evening? "That's life. No happiness without tears. No sorrow without a smile."

Else talks about her life in the Korngold residence.

"Erich is simply wonderful!" she gushes. "He plays piano all day long. He's currently composing the soundtrack to *The Sea Hawk*. It's a film about a naval battle between Spain and England. Very dramatic."

Sirius pricks up his ears. That sounds like the film he's acting in.

"And at lunchtimes he always gives me piano lessons," Else continues. "He's an absolute genius! He was eleven when he composed his first concerto, a piano piece for the ballet."

Erich Korngold and his wife, "Luzi," have two children, Ernst and Georg. They all live there together with the grandparents, Julius and Josefine, who fled Europe in November.

"Like us," says Carl.

"I'd like to live like that one day," gushes Else. "With my children, my husband, with all of you, all under one roof."

Andreas Cohn writes her heartfelt love letters. He wants to come here, as soon as he can.

"Do you still love him?" asks Rahel.

"Yes," says Else. "Very much."

The waiter brings a dish which is declared by all at the table to be a sensation: round, oven-baked slices of dough covered with cheese, tomatoes and ham. An Italian invention.

Georg talks enthusiastically about his lectures with the philosopher Bertrand Russell, who has recently started teaching at the university.

"I thought you were studying medicine," says his father in astonishment.

"I am," replies Georg. "But there's no harm in educating oneself more, is there?"

It turns out that there's a pretty girl in the philosophy seminar, who giggles adorably whenever Russell goes into raptures about his theories.

"What are you giggling about?" Russell once asked.

The girl's response: "If I knew that, I wouldn't be here."

Russell made her answer the topic of his next lecture.

Georg has already been to the movies with the girl, who is named Electra.

"Aha!" says his father.

"John Clark was in the film, by the way," says Georg. "*Battle of the Giants*, a war film."

"Oh, the war," sighs Rahel.

The waiter brings the dessert. *Cassata*, an Italian ice-cream cake with candied fruits.

Else says: "Korngold is utterly convinced that Mendelssohn will survive Hitler."

*

Carl Crown has been getting up in the mornings very happily of late. A curious development, which—according to Billy Wilder, if you remember—is a sign he has a dream. But what is it? He still doesn't know.

What could he dream about? He'd like to transform himself, but into whom? Who would he rather be than himself?

It was a difficult question.

Take Giovanni Clarizzo, for example. He was a fisherman in a Sicilian village, then he transformed himself into a life-guard in Hollywood, and now look at him—he's a movie star named John Clark.

Was that Giovanni's dream? Or was it fate?

Perhaps a person isn't even aware of what they dream, until one day their eyes open and they see that life itself is simply dreamlike?

These are all questions which are going through Carl Crown's mind on his morning drive to Beverly Hills. Sirius is with him again today.

Crown has now started to enter the palace with a relaxed, casual air, almost like a good friend of the household. And yet he has never exchanged a single word with Clark's family. He only ever sees the children from a distance, when they're feeding the flamingos or playing mini-golf or something of the sort. Only on one occasion was there any indication that there was a mother on the premises. She was lying back on a sun lounger on the pavilion by the lake, having her finger-nails manicured. Presumably, behind her large sunglasses, she was picturing the time when she was still Gloria Hayson.

But today is different.

"Hi," she says in a friendly tone. "I'm Gloria."

The children, Emily and Garfield, rush straight over to the dog.

"Can we play with him?" asks Emily.

Garfield takes a fork from the breakfast table and throws it onto the meadow in the hope that the dog will fetch it.

John Clark comes over. "Would you like to play with the children, Sirius?" he inquires, a little stiffly, in much the same way someone might ask a prime minister to dance.

Crown tries to lighten the mood. "Sirius, show them what you can do!"

Sirius pricks up his ears. He goes up on his hind legs, does a somersault and lands on his front paws.

The children are stunned into silence. First their eyes go wide in amazement, then they scream with delight.

"Daddy, Daddy!" they call. "Did you see that?"

Sirius repeats the performance.

The children are beside themselves. They shout with glee, clap their hands and hop all around Sirius.

Even John Clark throws up his arms and shouts: "Bravo!" Gloria smiles.

Emily and Garfield romp around on the meadow with Sirius. The parents watch and lean in close to each other.

"I haven't seen them this happy in a long time," whispers Gloria.

"Nor me," Clark whispers back.

A painter with no reservations about being kitsch would immediately immortalize this scene in oil paints and have it framed in gold. Man and wife, united in love. Children in the background, with dog.

Crown thinks: Well done, guardian angel.

He looks at John Clark, the family man. A reassuring yet unfamiliar sight. Almost impossible to believe that this is the same man who was plucking mambas from the vines in the Banana House.

Clark is wearing a high-cut, navy blue blazer with a white roll-neck sweater and gray gabardine trousers. His thick black hair is combed back with brilliantine and glistens in the sun.

Crown is surprised that he notices any of this.

Is his secret dream perhaps to be a tailor or a barber? Crazy. Maybe Hollywood drives a man crazy.

"Mama, come quickly!" calls Emily. "Look, Sirius can read!"

The book on the rattan lounger has reminded Sirius of his old showpiece. He flicks through page after page, then suddenly lowers his head down wearily onto the book and begins to snore.

"He thinks the book is boring!" cheers Garfield.

"It kind of gives me the heebie-jeebies," says Gloria.

"But why?" asks Clark.

"I don't know," she replies. "To me, Sirius seems like a human who has turned into a dog. Just look at the expression on his face."

Sirius lets them look deep into his eyes.

"It's like he understands every word we're saying," says Gloria. "Maybe he can even speak, but just doesn't want to."

Clark takes his wife in his arms and kisses her.

"You still believe in miracles," he laughs.

*

Time flies. Days with gray skies become more frequent. Winter jacket months are coming.

A hat comes in handy too. Even a scarf, on occasion.

The weeks in which everything rhymes have arrived. The songs being played on the radio suddenly contain words like "mistletoe" and "cinnamon."

Christmas is just outside the door.

Literally.

Outside every front door in Hollywood, an illuminated Father Christmas stands there jovially. His red coat and his reindeer sleigh seem particularly unnecessary; after all, it isn't snowing.

* * *

Rahel is feeling depressed. She misses Berlin. She misses the house. She misses the children. She misses her husband. She misses everything, actually. Often she doesn't see her husband for days on end. When he sets off in the mornings she's still asleep, and when he comes back at night she's already asleep.

Being lonely is a tiring business.

She no longer has Sirius as a source of comfort, either. Why would he want to be here, anyway, when it's much nicer elsewhere?

Carl probably thinks the same.

Rahel looks at the photo on her bedside table. What happened to the young woman with the dazzling smile? Who is the man next to her? Was that really Carl?

It's only been a year since they left. But to her it feels like a lifetime.

There are days when she doesn't speak a single word. When that happens, she can't stand it anymore and flees from the house.

Today is one of those days. She sets off and walks. In front of the drugstore, a man is selling Christmas trees.

"Christmas trees! Christmas trees!" he calls. "They make you happy. Better than any drug."

Rahel buys a tree.

A short while later it is standing in their tiny living room, but it doesn't make her happy. Nothing is as miserable as the sight of a bare Christmas tree in an empty room.

Things look very different in John Clark's house, of course.

The entire palace is illuminated with fairy lights, and a

huge star of Bethlehem gleams on top of the Christmas tree.

Carpenters have constructed a wooden stall that is clearly meant to represent the nativity scene. A real live donkey stands in front of it. Astoundingly, the life-size figures of Mary and Joseph are actually moving. On closer inspection it becomes clear that they are actors. Extras from Warner Bros., presumably.

Crown and Sirius are overwhelmed by the spectacle.

"Shhh," whispers John Clark, gesturing toward the nativity. "They're auditioning."

"What are those chairs in the hay?" asks Crown. "Are they for the Three Wise Men?"

Clark shakes his head. "No, for us. We'll sit there on Christmas Eve, and Bob Hope will read the nativity story."

Crown thinks to himself how wonderful it would be if John Clark were to add: "Why don't you come along?"

But he doesn't.

*

Not another word about Christmas. The festive season is over now, it was bleak, and the Crown family has resolved that everything will be okay.

The New Year begins cheerfully. Crown receives a bonus for his services as guardian angel, from Jack Warner himself, as well as a pay raise.

John Clark would say: "Let's go and have a drink!"

Carl says: "Rahel, my darling, let's go and get you some beautiful new clothes!"

* * *

They go to Saks in Beverly Hills, the newly opened branch of Saks Fifth Avenue in New York. The dress they pick out is a design by Elsa Schiaparelli. Narrow-waisted, padded shoulders, knee-length. The latest fashion.

"You look like Carole Lombard," gushes Carl.

The salesman whispers: "I don't mean to be indiscreet, but Clark Gable was in here recently, newly wed to Carole Lombard."

He makes a dramatic pause and fans the air with his hand.

"She bought the very same dress."

Carl suppresses a whoop of joy.

The new dress needs to be baptized. A Hollywood night follows which couldn't have been more wonderful even if John Clark had orchestrated it.

Dinner at Ciro's. Errol Flynn comes over to their table, nods toward Carl and says: "I know you. Aren't you the one with the funny dog?"

Then he bows in front of Rahel. "I do apologize, that was before. As of today I will ask: Aren't you the one with the beautiful wife?"

Rahel blushes.

A short while later he sends a bottle of champagne to their table, with a card saying "Love Errol."

After dinner, they go to the Garden of Allah. The air is scented with magnolia, even though it's only January.

Rahel sees the illuminated swimming pool in the palm tree garden. Lovers are cuddling up to each other on Hollywood swings, sipping at cocktails and smooching. The moon is high in the night sky.

"I want to go swimming!" cries Rahel.

"Why not?" answers Carl, pressing into her hands the swimming costume he has bought for her as a surprise. To the waiter he says: "Please show the lady the changing rooms, then bring us two daiquiris."

Then he jumps into the water. In his suit and tie.

Rahel is speechless. Is she dreaming?

It isn't long before a giggling couple are swimming in the pool, the man in evening attire, and the woman flings her bare arms around him and whispers: "Happy New Year!"

*

Sirius sees a truck driving past with a huge bone on it. *The Revenge of the Dinosaurs* is being filmed in Hall 7.

Bones, he thinks. Perhaps there's chicken in the canteen. He slinks off toward the kitchen exit. It won't hurt to have a sniff around and see what's on the menu today.

Two men are walking toward him. They stop and point.

"Look," says one.

"Yes, I see," says the other.

They step closer.

"Not bad," says one.

"Yeah, very good," says the other.

Sirius stares at them wide-eyed. What do the men want?

"Cook?" calls one through the kitchen window.

Sirius suddenly feels uneasy. Is it possible that the men suddenly have an appetite for dog meat?

"Cook!" calls the other. "Is this your dog?"

The cook shakes his head. "No, he belongs to John Clark, I think. Or his chauffeur."

"Thanks," say the men, walking away.

A short while later, Carl Crown is summoned to Tyrone Chester's office. The director is famous for films so sentimental that people need new tear ducts after watching them.

"I hear you have a dog," says Chester.

"Yes," answers Crown.

"We're looking for a dog at the moment," says Chester. "A cute dog. Is your dog cute?"

"I think so," answers Crown.

"The dog needs to melt hearts," says Chester. "Does your dog melt hearts?"

"He melts mine," says Crown.

"That's not enough," replies Chester. "He needs to melt the hearts of millions of viewers. Can he do that?"

"I don't know," says Crown.

"Okay, we'll give it a go," decides Chester. "From tomorrow. Fifty dollars for the week. What's his name?"

"Sirius," says Crown.

"Sirius," repeats Chester. "Like the star? That's a good sign."

*

The movie is about an unscrupulous con artist who plans to marry and fleece a rich widow, but her boundless love for him softens his heart, and in a moving plot twist he ends up caring for her when she becomes terminally ill.

"And the dog?" asks Crown.

"He belongs to the rich widow," explains Chester.

"What does he need to do?" asks Crown.

Chester waves his hand nonchalantly. "Not much. He's just there. Widows with dogs are more likable."

Fair enough.

"Scene one," calls Chester. "Let's give it a go."

In the living room set, dripping with wealth, is a seating area with numerous chairs. These emphasize the widow's solitude at the very first glance. There are tracks laid on the floor so that the cameraman can glide effortlessly on his podium from the long shots to the close-ups.

The widow takes her place on the couch, has a quick touch-up from the makeup artist and murmurs her lines to herself. Sirius is supposed to lie at her feet. No problem for him.

The spotlights go on.

"Action!" calls Chester.

The cameraman rolls first toward wealth, then toward solitude.

"What's the point of all this money if I don't have love?" sighs the widow.

"Cut!" cries Chester. "When she says the word 'love,' Sirius needs to sit up and look at her. Explain that to him."

"He understands already," says Crown in the background.

The scene is repeated. Sirius does as instructed. He doesn't want to come across as a know-it-all, but wouldn't it be even more moving if he were to lay his paw tenderly on the widow's arm as she says the word "love"?

On the second repetition, he decides to just do it. Chester is impressed. "Yes, exactly! That's it!"

Scene 2.

The widow flicks through the newspaper and stumbles across the announcement of an aristocratic gentleman who is looking for love, completely unaware that he's a con artist. She decides to answer the ad.

Sirius is to lie at her feet again.

"Action!" calls Chester.

"Who knows," sighs the widow. "Maybe he's the love of my life?"

Sirius thinks that it wouldn't be a bad idea if he were to growl a little at this point. As a kind of warning.

Chester is delighted: "Exactly! Good idea. The dog growls. As a kind of warning."

It isn't long before he starts to address his directions straight at Sirius.

"How about if you look sadly into the camera at the end of the scene?"

Sirius looks sadly into the camera. He also puts a trace of melancholy in his expression.

"Excellent!" calls Chester.

To Crown he says: "Sold! Sirius has the role."

*

From that moment on, Carl Crown no longer chauffeurs John Clark to the film studio, but Sirius instead.

"What a shame," says Clark. "Now I need to get by without a guardian angel. What will I do in the Banana House without you?"

"Be careful, that's what," Crown replies. "The problem with the mambas is that their poison immobilizes the heart muscles. It goes straight to your heart's core. That's why they're so dangerous."

Clark is flummoxed: "How do you know these things?"

"I was a biologist in my former life," replies Crown. "So, remember, be careful with your heart!"

"I'll try," laughs Clark.

Sirius is now the Hollywood star around which the Crowns' lives revolve. And yet he's not really a star. This is his very first film role. But he has an official ID from Warner Bros. on which it says: "Name: Sirius. Profession: Animal Actor."

Rahel gives him a good brush before he leaves the house every morning. "Give it your all!" she calls after him. "Remember everything you've learned!"

She sees little Levi before her. How he was trembling with fear when they found him. He had only just come into the world, and immediately his own world fell apart. He had to transform himself into a cushion in order to survive. And luck was on his side.

How smart he already was back then, Rahel thinks to herself.

When the cushion suddenly waved its tail, Levi was born again. He had already experienced enough to be able to understand the world.

Has he understood humans ever since that day?

The Big Dog constellation was in the sky back then, the only glimmer of light in the darkness. Levi transformed himself into a star, Sirius, and saved his family's life.

Only he who transforms himself survives.

Rahel is still in her dressing gown. It's ten in the morning. She smiles, opens the front door and steps out onto the street. Like Carl used to back then; every morning, always at ten on the dot, day after day.

She looks up to the sky. It's cloudless, a brilliant blue. The Big Dog is nowhere to be seen.

His star is currently rising in Hollywood. In Hall 2. In the film *A Widow Lives Twice*.

*

A phone call from Jack Warner's office.

The switchboard operator in Hall 2 walks on tiptoes so as not to disturb the filming.

"Mr. Crown," she whispers, "Jack Warner wants to see you."

* * *

Crown sets off on his way to the main building. In the elevator, he runs through his thank-you speech once again. On behalf of my family, he wants to say, I thank you—but then he's already being welcomed by the head secretary and taken to Jack Warner.

The mogul sits behind a desk which resembles a monumental coffin. The rest of the room, too, is wood-paneled.

"Look who it is!" he cries in greeting. "The man from Berlin. The guardian angel."

Crown clears his throat and begins: "In the name of my family . . ."

Jack Warner waves his hand. "No need for any of that. I called you here to talk about your dog. I hear you have a very interesting dog."

"Sirius?" asks Crown, pleased.

"Maybe," says Warner. "I'm not good with names. Even when I see that moody chap with the cigarette in the corner of his mouth, I have to think for a moment before I remember—ah yes, Humphrey Bogart."

He gestures for Crown to take a seat.

"But," Warner continues, "I know when talent crops up on the horizon. I can smell it from afar." He closes his eyes and sniffs. "I've got a good nose for talent. I saw a few scenes with your dog recently. He has talent. Incredible talent. He even has it in him to beat Skippy."

Skippy is the dog that has held the public's hearts ever since he played Asta in *The Thin Man*. He is Hollywood's biggest star on four legs. By now the terrier is earning more than most actors on two legs and leading the glamorous life of a film star. But Skippy is getting old. He's losing his enthusiasm. He wants to retire from the film business.

"Skippy's getting on my nerves," snorts Warner. "Apparently he feels 'sidelined.' The roles aren't 'demanding' enough for him. If you ask me he's become too full of himself. Right now he's in a bad mood because Orson Welles got the lead in *Citizen Kane* and not him. Just imagine!"

Crown tries to imagine it. Charles Foster Kane, played by Skippy.

He can't help but agree with Jack Warner.

"So," says the mogul, "here's the deal: two hundred dollars a week, for man and dog. After all, you belong together. We'll make a start after the summer."

Crown can't hold his hand out quickly enough. Two hundred dollars, that means that—thanks to Sirius—his weekly wage has doubled.

"Great," says Warner. "Where's the dog?"

"He's filming right now," answers Crown.

Warner's reply: "And? I always shake my stars' hands when I sign them up. In this case, his paw, of course."

He reaches for the telephone receiver and commands: "Get the dog here!"

Sirius appears soon after.

Jack Warner greets him with the same degree of respect he shows every artistic talent, regardless of whether they come in the door on two legs or four.

"Welcome to the Warner Bros. family!" he calls ceremoniously.

Sensing the good mood in the room, Sirius permits himself one of his beloved jokes for such occasions. He stands upright on his back legs and stretches out his right paw in salute.

Jack Warner stares at him in disbelief. Then he laughs so much he almost bursts.

"I'll have to tell Charlie Chaplin about that," he snorts. "It's incredible. Even better than *The Great Dictator*."

His laughter is still echoing along the corridor even once Crown and Sirius are out by the elevator.

Downstairs in the lobby, they run into John Clark.

"You two? Here?" asks Clark in surprise.

Crown tells him what has happened.

"Are you serious?" asks Clark, delighted. "That's unbelievable."

"Congratulations, my dear colleague!" he says to Sirius.

And to Crown, he of course says: "Let's go and have a drink."

*

An invitation to the big summer party—hosted by Earl and Linda Stein—is the highlight of the Hollywood party calendar.

Earl is founder of the most powerful artists agency; anyone who stands in front of the camera or sings into a microphone in America is represented by him.

This is easily confirmed by a glance at the guests getting out of their limousines this evening. Greta Garbo, Howard Hughes, Joan Crawford, Clark Gable, Bing Crosby, Ingrid Bergman, Cary Grant. Everyone is there.

The Crowns have been invited too, even though they don't know the Steins. But the grapevine moves fast in Hollywood. The mysterious dog, recently signed by Jack Warner, naturally belongs on the guest list.

Skippy has withdrawn his RSVP. He has no intention of going if any old mongrel is invited.

The real motive for the party is so that Linda Stein, known as "Queenie," can prove once more that she's the party queen of Hollywood. She greets the guests on the red carpet.

"Clark, my darling!" she cries. "You were so wonderful in *Gone With the Wind*. Really spectacular!"

Clark Gable bows. "Thank you, Queenie."

A rumor is going around Hollywood that he only took on the role of Rhett Butler in order to pay his astronomical dental bills. He really wanted to do *Tarzan*, but the movie slipped through his fingers.

"Elsa Schiaparelli!" screeches Queenie, catching a glimpse of Carole Lombard's dress. Then she whispers quietly: "You must tell me where you got it."

"Saks, in Beverly Hills," Carole whispers back. "Just between you and me."

* * *

Suddenly Queenie sees an animal on the red carpet. "Sirius!" she rejoices, haughtily ignoring his significant others. Rahel wishes the floor could swallow her up. She is wearing the exact same dress as Carole Lombard. So the salesman wasn't fibbing.

In the garden, the guests are awaited by tables set out in a star formation around a dance floor. There is an illuminated podium in the middle, where Guy Lombardo and his orchestra are playing the hits of the season.

A short man with a hat perched askew approaches the Crowns. It's that dancing Austrian again, Billy Wilder.

"How are you?" inquires Crown.

"Nobody is perfect," replies Wilder, noticing that this still doesn't quite work as a punch line.

Sirius only has to look at the buffet for some attentive waiter to nod and load up a plate with things that dogs might like.

"Shrimps?" asks the waiter uncertainly.

Sirius scrunches up his nose.

"Shrimps are good," advises Cary Grant.

"Cocktail sausages are better," adds Fred Astaire.

Carl sits next to a young actress who introduces herself as Hedy Lamarr. It takes a good while before both of them realize that they can speak to each other in German. Hedy is actually named Hedwig Kiesler and is from Austria. She complains about the fact that everyone just stares at her cleavage, when she actually happens to be developing a frequency-hopping process for mobile communications technology. The invention came about when she and the composer George Antheil were trying to synchronize one of his works for sixteen mechanical pianos. General Motors is interested in patenting it.

Carl Crown prefers to stare at her cleavage.

"You're doing the right thing," says John Clark, clapping him on the shoulder. "There's nothing more beautiful than the Hollywood Hills."

Rahel is amusing herself at the cocktail bar, surrounded by a group of young Italians. Their shirts gape open to reveal glinting crucifixes dangling down over their torsos. They wear sunglasses even at night.

The rumor is going around that Earl Stein, the host, is pressuring the stars into making appearances in his friend Al Capone's nightclubs.

The orchestra plays "Summertime." George Gershwin, the song's composer, and his wife, Lee, step onto the dance floor, closely intertwined.

The guests applaud.

Crown is just about to get up and ask Rahel to dance when he is drawn into a conversation about Eisenstein with a screenplay writer. He watches from the corner of his eye as Rahel dances with one of the Italians instead. The man seems to be funny; Rahel is throwing her head back and laughing heartily. What about? Could it be the latest joke from Calabria? Or an anecdote from day-to-day life with Al Capone? He is certainly a good dancer, you have to give him that.

* * *

Sirius sits on the lap of a woman who has wrapped a servi-
ette around his neck so that he looks respectable while
enjoying his dessert.

By midnight, the Italian is singing too. He scales the podium
and performs a song with the title "I'll Never Smile Again,"
giving it his all.

"Who is that guy?" asks Crown.

"He's named Frankie," says Rahel. "That's all I know."

Crown lights himself a cigarette. He took up smoking
recently. Life feels more exciting when you have something
burning in your hand.

It burns time too. You light it up, suck it in, breathe it out.

That's probably how it goes with fame, reflects Crown.
But he doesn't have time to ponder that thought any further,
for suddenly Dolores del Río is standing in front of him,
asking for a light.

*

Other than that, the summer is under the spell of the third
movement of Mendelssohn's Violin Concerto, op. 64.

The fulfillment of great love.

Andreas Cohn has finally arrived. There he stands, on
the station platform, with his violin case in his hand. His
luggage is just being unloaded.

Else sobs with happiness as they fall into each other's
arms. Almost two years have passed since they last saw each
other.

Andreas looks into the faces which have burned themselves into his memory and slowly faded, like photographs from days gone by. Now, all of a sudden, new life has been breathed into them. They return his gaze, they smile back, they speak.

New life.

Else is no longer a delicate little creature with angelic locks. She wears her hair short now, and her sun-bronzed skin is scented with sunshine and swimming pools. She has become a young woman.

Carl is barely recognizable. He looks like a film star in his white suit, chic silk scarf and casual straw hat—is this really the same man who was awarded the golden Cothenius Medal for his services at the microscope?

Georg looks more like Carl every day. The Carl from back then, that is. He has inherited the reserved seriousness that his father has clearly left behind him. Even though Georg hasn't graduated yet, one could easily call him "Herr Doktor" already. Although maybe that also has something to do with the horn-rimmed glasses he recently started wearing.

Rahel has blossomed. Her breezy yellow dress gleams like a sunflower. Did she always used to accentuate her pouting lips with red lipstick? Just like before, she is still fond of sighing.

"Oh, Andreas," she sighs.

Andreas looks just the same as everyone remembers him. The lean, tall figure, the black locks framing his pale face and dark, angry eyes. The very opposite of a sonny boy, as they say in Hollywood.

The black floor-length coat darkens his aura even more. The people on the station platform stare at the eerie arrival from Europe. They will see him again in the autumn, when he starts to play the violin in the Los Angeles Philharmonic Orchestra. Signed by Otto Klemperer.

Sirius greets Andreas. He circles him with his tail wagging, then snuffles at his bag.

"That's right," laughs Andreas. "I brought you something. For all of you, in fact. Just a little something."

He unpacks a box of biscuits.

Everyone from Basel is incredibly proud of their city's baked delicacy. It's a kind of *Lebkuchen* which is particularly hard and chewy. The recipe originates from the seventeenth century, and one could be forgiven for thinking that the biscuits have been in the box ever since. Sirius is still chewing on his even by the time the fully laden Chevrolet turns into Melrose Avenue.

"Welcome to Hollywood!" cries Carl.

Andreas is startled when he walks into the tiny wooden house that Carl and Rahel live in. The last time he saw them they lived in a town house which was sometimes mentioned in the same breath as the Sistine Chapel. With a little stretch of the imagination, of course.

Overall, his first impressions aren't great. The long journey, the big city, the new language, the strange new world. And particularly the new Liliencrons.

He will stay with Georg initially. Carl wants to show him the city. Rahel wants to hear the latest news from Europe. And he simply must accompany Sirius into the film studio. Erich Korngold is looking forward to meeting him.

But for now, Andreas belongs to Else.

*

A Widow Lives Twice is being premiered.

Hollywood Boulevard has been closed off. The onlookers throng toward the Chinese Theatre, where the red carpet has been laid out. Everyone wants to see the stars.

Spotlights shine high up into the sky, circling their beams of light. Cameramen, photographers and reporters line the streets. One black limousine after another drives past. Premiere guests, too impatient to wait, climb out and push their way toward the throng on foot.

Some of them have a packet of Kleenex in their handbags. It's advisable when Tyrone Chester is the director.

Flashbulbs glitter as the widow steps onto the red carpet, accompanied by the con artist. Hands stretch toward them, accompanied by pleas for autographs.

Then the door of the next limousine opens, the chauffeur bows and a dog gets out.

A storm of camera flashes.

"Sirius! Sirius!" scream the photographers.

The widow reacts with the speed of a lightning bolt. She picks up the dog and poses for the cameras.

*   *   *

By the time Tyrone Chester walks onto the red carpet and links arms with the abandoned con artist, the camera flashes have long since been turned off. And by the time Carl and Rahel arrive, the cameramen are no longer to be seen. The couple come at the very last minute and are lucky to be allowed into the cinema. Carl has rented himself a tuxedo, while Rahel is hoping that she won't run into Carole Lombard again.

The lights in the room dim, the screen shines brightly.

Sirius looks as big as a horse when he appears, taking his place by the widow's feet.

He lays his colossal paw on her monumental arm—and the audience sobs.

"The dog really understands her," whimpers an elderly woman next to Rahel.

When Sirius warns the widow with his growl, the man next to Carl wipes the sweat from his brow: "Thank God!"

The film seems to be having the desired impact on its audience.

But it's still a failure with the critics.

The *Hollywood Reporter* writes: "As a viewer, you can't help but wish that the widow had only lived once. Or better still: not at all."

The film critic from the *New York Times* says: "There was only one excellent actor in this film, and he had four legs."

*   *   *

The next morning, the picture of the widow with the dog is on all the front pages.

"Look," says Rahel proudly to Sirius as they walk past the kiosk. "That's you!"

The kiosk woman stares at them. So intensely that her eyes become two narrow slits.

A few days later, when the two of them walk by again, she calls out to Rahel: "I saw the movie. It's strange how the dog looks much smaller in real life."

*

After just a few weeks, there are posters hanging all over Hollywood: "If you like Skippy, you'll love Sirius!"

Beneath those words is a likeness of Sirius, drinking a milkshake with a cheeky smile.

Jack Warner knows the business well. He seizes the moment.

Advertising posters bang the drum for the widow who lives twice—and hopefully even longer at the box office—and start to pique people's curiosity about the next film with the "biggest star of the dog world."

Sirius plays "Hercules," the loyal companion of a courageous family of settlers who, while seeking their fortune in the Wild West, are confronted by all manner of adverse situations. The father is sheriff of the small backwater town.

Jack Warner wants John Wayne for the role.

"Are you insane?" blusters Wayne. "I hate dogs!"

Warner tries to simplify things for a temperament that is already simple enough.

"But the dog isn't a dog at all. He's a hero! He repeatedly rescues the family from all manner of adverse situations."

Wayne is not calmed down by this, quite the contrary.

"I'm the hero!" he screams. "If anyone is going to rescue the family from all manner of adverse situations, then it's me. And on a horse. Not with a dog."

"Matt McDaniel is the director!" rejoices Warner. His expression implies that he is bringing the trump card into play.

John Wayne hesitates: "The Negro?"

"What are you talking about?" says Warner. "You mean *Hattie* McDaniel, the actress. No, Matt McDaniel is a man, and white."

"Well, there's that at least," grumbles Wayne.

The negotiations are adjourned.

Jack Warner is under pressure. Autumn is already approaching. The brilliant blue sky, beneath which the family of settlers are supposed to seek their fortune, will soon be gone. Heaven forbid that they have to film in winter. Then the family would have to shovel snow, and artificial snow at that, in the studio. That would be expensive.

But that's exactly what happens.

John Wayne turns the role down. And negotiations with Errol Flynn fall through too. The screenplay has to be completely rewritten. The settlers now have the weather to contend with as well. In the end, an actor named Morton

Wilcox gets the role. Not the catchiest of names. But it doesn't matter; after all, the true star is Sirius.

The studio grounds are being transformed into the Wild West. Hills are heaped up and forested. Prairie grass and pebbles are transported in. Rocks tower up from the steppe. The poor settlers; they'll have to dig it all up again and make it fertile.

A town is being constructed. All just facades, of course. A weather-beaten sign bears the name "Luckyville." The cowboys will ride through the dusty main street. Sinister strangers will arrive at the train station. Guns will smoke in the saloon.

Luckily, the sheriff and Hercules are on hand to keep law and order in this "goddamn backwater."

*

Sirius is trembling all over. His pulse is racing. He rolls his eyes. He whimpers. And all because some drunken cattle handler has just fired a shot at the ceiling in the saloon.

"Cut!" calls the director.

According to the script, Hercules is now supposed to dash off to the farm and get the sheriff's help. But he can't. He flees to the farthest corner of the studio and cowers there, the picture of misery. Crown picks him up.

"What's wrong?" asks the director.

Crown is completely baffled. "I don't know."

"Has this ever happened before?" asks the director.

"No," replies Crown. "But why would it have? We don't fire guns at home."

The settlers look at each other, taken aback. Some giggle. The dog they call Hercules is easily spooked.

It's a catastrophe.

There's nothing else for it, Sirius has to see a psychiatrist. And quickly.

That very same day, Dr. Robert Methusalem takes on the case. He's considered an expert.

Sirius lies down on the couch.

"What happened?" asks Dr. Methusalem.

Crown describes the events, starting with Luckyville, the drunken cattle handler in the saloon, the gunshots.

"Gunshots?" interrupts Dr. Methusalem.

Sirius shakes just upon hearing the word.

"I suspect early childhood trauma," murmurs Dr. Methusalem.

Crown continues, journeying back to Berlin, back to the night when the synagogue was burning and the streets were filled with mountains of shards, caretaker Zinke on the truck, gasoline, glass, gunshots, screams.

Dr. Methusalem makes notes. He raises his eyebrows slightly when the word "gunshots" comes up again.

Crown describes the zero hour: Levi had just come into the world when the men in boots came, shooting all the dogs except one—him.

"There we have it!" cries Dr. Methusalem. "Post-traumatic stress disorder. It's a clear-cut case."

* * *

"Terrible," says Crown. He hugs Sirius tightly against him. "I thought you had long forgotten all of that."

Sirius closes his eyes. He doesn't want anyone to see his tears.

"Forgotten?" corrects Dr. Methusalem. "Suppressed, more like!

"Sometimes," he continues, "the trauma even induces a personality change. The soul wants to protect itself, to ensure it's never hurt again. The personality becomes highly sensitive, almost hypersensitive. Have you noticed anything like that?"

"Yes," replies Crown, "we have."

"It doesn't necessarily have to be a disadvantage," says Dr. Methusalem. "Mozart was traumatized. And look what became of him."

Sirius has fallen asleep.

"And now?" asks Crown. "What should we do?"

"There are two options," declares Dr. Methusalem. "I once had a patient who was a war veteran. Extremely traumatized. A heavy stutterer. So I shot at him with a blank pistol in our sessions. For two years, and then he was healed."

"And the second option?" asks Crown.

"Very simple," replies Dr. Methusalem. "Avoid gunshots." With a wink, he adds: " I mean, we all avoid gunshots. It's completely normal."

"How are we supposed to manage that?" asks Crown in despair. "My dog is playing the lead role in a Western! They're always firing guns. He's playing Hercules, a dog that knows no fear."

Dr. Methusalem: "Just put a little cotton wool in his ears. That's what I do when my wife gets too loud."

Crown goes back to the film studio, a few insights the richer. On the way, he buys some cotton wool.

"So?" asks the director. "Problem solved?"

"I think so, yes," replies Crown.

"Great," says the director. "Then let's continue. Listen up, everyone! We'll shoot scene twelve now. The shoot-out at the train station. Props team, bring the weapons please!"

Sirius defies the hailstorm of bullets as fearlessly and invulnerably as only a Hercules can.

*

Life in Luckyville has a happy ending, of course.

Hercules and the sheriff can breathe a sigh of relief. There are no more adverse situations to confront. The settlers have found the happiness they were seeking in the Wild West. Even though the weather was bad at times. But even when it was, they still had a roof over their heads—in Hall 1. Hollywood looks after people who have a dream.

Now only the final scene remains.

"Christmas Eve!" cries the director.

All the residents of Luckyville gather around a big Christmas tree and sing "O Christmas Tree" together.

"Snow!" cries the director.

Artificial snow flutters down gently from the skies.

This was exactly the expense that Jack Warner had wanted to avoid, but even he has to hold back a tear.

Applause. The dream factory has done a good job.

Reality lies in wait for the residents of Luckyville. They return to their real lives, to their little worlds, to their own adverse situations.

The sheriff has just separated from his wife.

"Then come to us for Christmas Eve!" says Crown.

Fate isn't shy about handing out a few surprises. This year, Sirius will celebrate Christmas with the sheriff twice.

"Santa Claus Is Coming to Town" is playing on the radio. A new Christmas song at last.

"Christmas trees! Christmas trees!" cries the seller in front of the drugstore. "They make you happy. Better than any drug."

Rahel smiles. This time he's right. For the Crown family, the year drawing to a close has been a good one.

In a way, they too are settlers who have found their happiness in the Wild West.

*

Adolf Hitler sees the end of the year as an opportunity to give a speech in the Berlin Sportpalast:

"And so we enter the New Year with a Wehrmacht armed more powerfully than we have ever seen in our country's history."

"*Sieg Heil!*" cries the audience.

"1941," he continues, "will be the decisive year for a great New Order in Europe!"

"*Sieg Heil!*" cries the audience.

"And another thing," he adds, "the Duce and I, we are neither Jews nor are we profiteers. When we shake hands, it is the handshake of men of honor."

The German Reich now includes Poland, Denmark, Norway, Holland, Yugoslavia and Greece. France is occupied. Italy is an ally. In the Reich Chancellery, preparation for the Russian campaign is under way.

Far away from war-related events, a little dog called Sirius is conquering Hollywood.

But he neither attacked nor fought. He simply sat in front of a kitchen door in the hope that a few chicken bones might be going begging—and the rest is history. In this decisive year.

Sirius is now Hercules.

The film poster shows the sheriff arresting some sinister baddie, while in the foreground Hercules is ready and waiting with the handcuffs.

"Thank Heaven for Hercules," says the caption.

The poster is all over Hollywood. In front of Grauman's Chinese Theatre, where the premiere is to be held, *Hercules* is even stretched across Hollywood Boulevard. The dog is so huge that the cars heading in one direction drive through the right handcuff, and the contraflow through the left.

* * *

High above Hollywood, a Hercules-shaped hot air balloon hovers in the sky, as if the dog were the landmark of the city. In the long history of zoology, there has probably never been a dog that got so much attention.

Sirius now has an agent who takes care of his public relations. Her name is Iris Green, and it's her job to make sure Hercules receives "the attention he deserves," as Jack Warner puts it.

"How about a nice dinner at the Romanoff tonight?" Miss Green suggests. "At the invitation of Mr. Warner, of course."

Romanoff is the new restaurant on Rodeo Drive. It's the talk of the town, and the Romanoff steak is supposed to be excellent, but the real attraction is the chef, a gentleman who is claiming to be Prince Michael Dimitri Alexandrovich Obolensky-Romanoff. Whether that's his real name or not is anyone's guess.

"Hercules," says Prince Obolensky-Romanoff with a bow as the Crowns walk in with Sirius on the lead.

"Table four," he calls to the waiter.

All eyes in the room are on Hercules.

Skippy is sitting at Table 3.

All conversations in the room fall silent.

Skippy growls. He doesn't just see another dog on his territory, but the dog through whose handcuffs he has to drive day after day whenever he wants to go downtown, and it's the same dog who is floating over Hollywood, filled with hot air.

Skippy hates this dog. He jumps down from his seat so

speedily that his companion cries out in surprise. Then he stalks over to the enemy and obstructs his path in a threatening manner.

Sirius too has pulled away from his lead and is baring his teeth.

There they stand, opposite each other, in the middle of the Romanoff: Skippy, the King of Hollywood, and Hercules, his contender.

The guests get up from their tables. Some even clamber up onto their chairs to get a better view. To be on the safe side, the waiters hold the trays laden with Romanoff steaks up above their heads.

Skippy attacks. He launches himself at Hercules, ramming his head into his flank, snapping for his neck. Hercules catches Skippy by the tail, hurls him up into the air, then flings him down to the floor. Then the two dogs roll, locked together, escaping for a brief moment only to stalk around each other again moments later.

As if by magic, photographers have appeared. As they snap their pictures, the dogs flicker in the storm of flashbulbs.

Miss Green smiles. She knows how happy Jack Warner will be when he opens the morning papers tomorrow. And she's right.

"Battle in the Romanoff!" says the headline of the *Hollywood Reporter*.

"Dual of the Giants," says the *Los Angeles Times*.

Both dogs are unharmed, but Hercules is the clear victor.

* * *

On the day of the film premiere, Sirius makes an especially dramatic appearance: he is limping a little as he makes his way down the red carpet, and his right front paw is bandaged. As a sign of heroism. It was no easy ascent to the top. He had to fight for it.

The onlookers' hearts are won. Sirius is now conclusively a star.

*

Hercules is a box office smash. People flock to the movie theaters to see the dog that takes care of law and order in the Wild West.

The dog doesn't speak one single word in the film, and only once is his shrewd expression accompanied by a sonorous voice: "I'm wilder than the West, and that's a fact." Upon hearing this, the crook puts his Colt in his holster and backs away.

The line swiftly becomes a catchphrase in America.

It can be heard in playgrounds, in bars, in offices, at parties. It's almost impossible for a woman to be flirted with without the man lowering his voice and saying: "I'm wilder than the West, and that's a fact."

Even Franklin D. Roosevelt, the president of the United States, utters the words in jest during an after-dinner speech at the White House.

Hercules is on everyone's lips.

Jack Warner relaxes back into his chair. He realizes, however, that it just won't do for his star to be living in a wooden shack anymore. How will that look to the reporters who are already queuing up to be permitted to visit Hercules on his home territory?

He instructs Miss Green to find a prestigious home for the Crowns.

"It has to make a statement," he says. "Villa Hercules."

Miss Green gets to work. Her favorite is a house that was built just recently. It perches on a cliff and has a view of the whole of Hollywood. In actual fact, the entire house is constructed solely from glass.

Jack Warner looks at the photos, shaking his head. "What on earth is it? Is it supposed to be a house?"

"It's modern!" gushes Miss Green. "Very interesting architecture."

"Hercules is interesting enough by himself," replies Warner belligerently. "People are supposed to talk about the dog, not the house."

"The house is unique," Miss Green continues to gush. "As unique as Hercules."

"Mm-hmm," grumbles Warner. "There's a bit too much glass. For a dog. Doesn't that seem strange?"

"Not in the slightest!" exclaims Miss Green. "When Hercules sits by the window, his silhouette will become one with the backdrop of the city. Hercules and Hollywood, one and the same."

"That sounds good," murmurs Warner. "Perhaps the two of us should live in the house, and then our silhouettes can become one with the backdrop of the city."

"Mr. Warner!" cries Miss Green indignantly.

* * *

And so the rental contract is signed. The young architect, John Lautner, furnishes the rooms in the spirit of modernity. But he refuses to erect a rustic wooden sign with the inscription "Villa Hercules" at the entrance.

When the Crowns catch their first glimpse of their new home, they are speechless.

Modernist minimalism isn't yet a concept they are familiar with. They stand there in the glass cube and gape like people who have just landed on a foreign planet.

Carl gives a start when he sees that an abyss opens up just beyond the window, the ground only appearing again far below in the valley.

Sirius hears the echo of his steps in the high-ceilinged living area.

"Isn't it a bit too big for us?" asks Rahel.

"Think of the photographers, the reporters," Miss Green assures her. "It'll soon fill up, you'll see."

And it does. The house fills up, day after day, hour after hour. The doorbell rings relentlessly, and one curious visitor after another steps in.

"Villa Hercules," crows the female reporter from *House & Garden.* "I never would have expected a Western hero to live in such modern surroundings!"

Rahel requests politely that she remember to differentiate between the dog and the role.

"Does Hercules love modern architecture?" the reporter wants to know.

"Absolutely," responds Rahel. "He's an aesthete."

"How darling!" giggles the reporter.

The photographer from *Gourmet* magazine wants to photograph Hercules while he's eating.

"What's his favorite dish?" he asks.

"Turkey goulash with tagliatelle," Rahel dreams up.

"Does he like filet mignon too?" asks the photographer. "Because that's what I prepared in advance. For the photo."

The columnist from *Life* lies down with Hercules on the couch. The name of her column is "Five Questions on the Couch."

"Can you sing too?" asks a radio reporter.

Hercules yowls "Y'a d'la joie" by Maurice Chevalier.

The cameraman from Pathé News films the house from outside for their newsreel. "Can we do an interview in the garden later?"

"I just need five minutes for a caricature," interrupts the caricaturist from *The New Yorker*.

"Is Hercules interested in fashion?" asks the editor of *Vogue*. "He sure is!" answers Rahel.

The columnist of the *Boston Globe* wants to talk to Hercules about Boston.

"Does Hercules like Boston?"

Carl jumps in: "He loves Boston."

"I can't work like this!" bellows the art photographer. "I have to concentrate! I need peace and quiet!"

* * *

Peace and quiet? They don't exist in this house anymore.

Sirius is exhausted by all the questions he's suddenly being confronted with. Does Hercules like Boston? He's never been to Boston. And he's not Hercules.

It's all very confusing. The reporters have left now, and Sirius is alone, with his questions.

"Who am I?" he wonders. And: "Am I happy?"

These questions. These eternal questions.

Sirius goes over to the window, and his silhouette becomes one with the backdrop of Hollywood.

*

In the spring, Jack Warner gives the green light for a *Hercules* sequel: *Hercules Returns.*

In the summer, filming will already begin for the sequel to the sequel: *Hercules: One Against All.*

Warner is spinning the wheel of happiness at ever-increasing speeds.

Sirius really doesn't know how he is supposed to manage all of this. Hercules is starting to get on his nerves. The dog is constantly stumbling into some new adventure and dragging Sirius along with him. After the demanding spell in the Wild West, it would have been nice to take a little breather, but instead Hercules is returning already!

Sirius also can't figure out the criteria by which Hercules selects his adventures. Why does he now have to fight against pirates who are making trouble on the island of "Hula" in the South Pacific? The natives are distraught, of course; their princess has been kidnapped and most probably by cannibals, and only Hercules can save the day.

He does, and very gallantly too. The film is almost a wrap.

But after that, the journey will continue to Rome, where Emperor Nero is threatening to set the city on fire if someone doesn't come forward with the Temple's golden chest, which was stolen by the Vestal Virgins, and again Hercules is the only one who can save the day.

Saving the day has its limits, thinks Sirius. He's at the end of his strength. He's barely eating anymore. He's not sleeping well.

The Crowns are very worried.

Georg, who by now is in his fifth semester of medicine, makes a decisive diagnosis: "Stress."

"What's that?" asks Rahel.

"It's a new phenomenon," replies Georg. "Sensory overload. Professor Hans Selye is in the process of researching it. He calls it "'stress.'"

Georg prescribes, for the time being, a complete lack of excitement.

"Switzerland would be the ideal place in that respect, naturally," he ponders. "But that's out of the question. So absolute rest will have to suffice."

Crown speaks to Jack Warner, who—as expected—flies off the handle.

"Rest? How can we manage that?"

Crown pleads for his understanding: "The dog is at the breaking point with his nerves. His hair is even falling out."

Warner waves his hand dismissively: "Then he's no different from me."

He agonizes for a moment, then says: "Okay, I'll add another one hundred dollars a week."

It's only when Crown rejects the offer that he realizes the severity of the situation, and shakes his head sadly.

"The Colosseum, the gladiator costumes," he mumbles, "and all for nothing. Such a pity."

But he gives in: "Okay then. Give my canine friend my best wishes for his recovery."

Tranquillity arrives in the Crown household.

Sirius lies quietly by the open window. A gentle breeze ruffles his fur. He listens to his heart beating.

Rahel and Carl walk around on tiptoes. When they speak to each other, they whisper.

Even the birds, when they fly high in the air past the strange glass nest, try to flap their wings as quietly as they can.

Their wings are flapping to the same rhythm as my heartbeat, thinks Sirius. What does that mean?

He remembers the 30-million-year-old duck, back in Berlin. In his mind he wanders through the Tiergarten, back to the tree on Klamtstrasse. *His* tree.

Does the tree ever wonder what became of the dog that used to visit him every day?

"I work in a dream factory—imagine that!" Sirius would say to him if they saw each other again.

"A dream factory? What's that?" asks the tree.

Sirius tells him about Hula, Luckyville and the widow who only just escaped being the victim of a con artist.

"But that sounds awful," says the tree. "Who would have dreams like that?"

"Humans," says Sirius.

"Humans," repeats the tree, shaking his crown sadly. "You look exhausted. Can I give you some advice?"

"Of course," replies Sirius. "That's why I came."

"Don't worry, just live!" says the tree. "Positive thinking."

*

Else had admittedly already mentioned that she was going to bring a little something along on her next visit, but the amazement on her parents' faces is still considerable when they see what it is.

A huge black concert piano.

It takes four men to heave it into the house. "Now that's what I call a little something," says Carl.

Rahel is speechless.

"Korngold gave me the Steinway," says Else. "As a good-bye present."

"Good-bye?" asks Rahel.

Else smiles: "I'm pregnant."

Is there anything more thrilling for parents than a concert piano which delivers this kind of news? Carl and Rahel embrace their daughter, overwhelmed with emotion.

Even the four men still waiting for their tip have tears in their eyes.

"Let's have a party!" cries Rahel.

An excellent idea.

"We do party planning too," say the four men in chorus.

That very same day ushers in an unforgettable evening. The glass house has been transformed beyond recognition. Any birds flying by right now could easily think they've detoured to Hong Kong by mistake.

One of the four party planners, a Chinese man and clearly the decorator of the quartet, has illuminated the terrace with lanterns made from red tissue paper. The lantern, he explains, is a symbol of fertility.

There are bulbs of garlic all over the place. To bring luck for the birth of a son. And mandarins too, in case it should be a girl.

By the entrance stand torches which smell of sulfur. They are to scare away the demons.

Luckily there is something decent to eat and drink too.

Georg comes with Electra. She is now his girlfriend. The Korngolds are there. And the sheriff, of course. John Clark, alone, for he has recently left his wife.

Carl lifts his glass to toast Else and Andreas.

"You learned to love each other during our family's darkest hour," he says, "and your love has now given us the brightest day of our lives. We thank you both for that," he continues, hand in hand with Rahel. "Your old family wishes your young family all the luck in the world."

"Good luck!" everyone cries.

The Chinese man hands each of the guests a nail. The symbol for the succession of generations.

Erich Korngold sits down at the piano and plays songs by Cole Porter. Everyone knows "Night and Day," sung by Fred Astaire, but when the sheriff suddenly strikes up the melody and sings, the song becomes even closer to people's hearts. Soon even John Clark is joining in at the top of his voice. And it doesn't take long before everyone is singing and dancing.

"Hey, Crown!" calls a voice.

There he is again, the strange Austrian with the cocked hat. He's dancing with Else.

Carl rubs his eyes in astonishment.

The hat means that Peter Lorre can't be far away. And sure enough, he has just arrived.

"We're late, I know," Lorre apologizes. "Billy got us lost."

"Nobody's perfect," winks Billy. The line has improved.

"Unbelievable," says Lorre. "Hercules is making more at the box office than me. You should be paying me a commission. After all, it was me who brought you all here!"

Carl thanks him awkwardly.

"Just a little joke," says Lorre.

Billy reports that Marlene Dietrich makes the best fried potatoes and scrambled eggs. "Marlene should have done the cooking tonight," he declares, "not the Chinese."

* * *

Where is Sirius anyway? Sometimes he's here, sometimes he's there. That's how it is when there's company. One person strokes him, another hands him a nibble. It's a lovely thing to be a dog in a happy house.

The "new life" in Hollywood—it hasn't even been that long yet and already there are "old times." The Korngolds think back to their time with Else. John Clark misses his guardian angel. The sheriff waxes lyrical about Luckyville.

Strangely, no one notices the dark clouds hanging over the house, perhaps because they seem to be coming from the barbecue in the garden.

But appearances can be deceiving.

The Chinese man knows better. Smoke means *change*, and clouds mean *big change*.

*

"Has my friend recovered?" asks Jack Warner.

"I think so," says Crown. "He's doing better."

Sirius is pleased by the expression of concern.

Warner didn't call them both over to his office to be compassionate, but he tries to see things from Sirius's perspective for a moment longer before he comes to the point.

"What kind of life is it?" he ruminates. "Always being in front of the camera—it's annoying, isn't it?"

Sirius pricks up his ears.

"The dream world," he continues, leaning back in his chair. "You want to get out into real life, the real world at last, right?"

Sirius stares at him, wide-eyed.

PART 2

Jack Warner comes to the point: "Yesterday, John Ringling North called me. He owns the biggest circus in the world, Ringling Bros. and Barnum & Bailey. He wants Hercules!"

Crown is speechless, Sirius likewise.

"Hercules—live!" rejoices Warner. "Just imagine: Hercules, the star of 'The Greatest Show on Earth!' That's the name of his tour."

Sirius looks as though he's not grasping the scale of the opportunity, so Warner adds: "You'll be sniffing circus air! You'll travel the world! Be among animals!" He corrects himself: "Animals? Not just any old animals. Jumbo, the king of the elephants. Gargantua, the famous gorilla!"

Sirius is certainly keen on the idea of playing with other animals more often, but does it really have to be a gorilla?

Warner guesses his thoughts and, to encourage him, tells him Gargantua's story. Ten years ago, the gorilla was captured in the Congo and ended up in the possession of an eccentric old woman in Brooklyn named Gertrude Lintz. She had another gorilla too, as well as numerous chimpanzees, and treated the monkeys like they were her own children. They wore made-to-measure clothes, ate dinner at the table, and even joined her for walks around the city.

"Isn't that amazing?" Warner says with delight.

Gargantua got bigger and bigger, and eventually he weighed four hundred pounds and no longer fit into the house. Gertrude Linz sold him to Ringling Bros. and Barnum & Bailey. Since then, the circus has billed him as "the world's most dangerous gorilla."

"Oh, the magic of the circus ring," sighs Warner. "The tent, the artists, the clowns, the magicians, the wild animals. And right in the midst of it all: Hercules."

Sirius has to admit that the idea has a certain appeal.

"And another thing," says Warner. "Direct contact with the public. The expressions of amazement on their faces. Children's laughter. The applause."

Crown is wondering what Jack Warner is up to. He's not the kind of man to give up *Hercules Part III* just because he wants a dog to experience the magic of the circus ring.

"I didn't know you were a fan of the circus," says Crown.

"I'm not," replies Warner. "It smells funny in the tent, and I get claustrophobic."

But—this is good business in the making. As an example, he explains the Clark Gable deal. Selznick, the producer of *Gone With the Wind*, wanted Gable at all costs, but he was under contract with MGM. So he had to borrow him, and of course the sum that MGM got from Selznick was higher than the fee MGM was contracted to pay Gable.

"Do you see?" beams Warner. "This is how we do things in Hollywood."

Crown sees. And Sirius can't hide the fact that he feels flattered to be mentioned in the same breath as Clark Gable.

But Warner promptly puts a damper on the comparison. "Clark Gable had bad breath. Because of his decaying teeth, you see. It was really bad. That's why he agreed to the deal only on the condition that he could earn a share of the profits and finally have money for the dentist."

Well, sometimes masterpieces arise from the strangest of circumstances.

"So," says Warner. "Let's talk turkey. The tour lasts six months. After that, Hercules will come back, and we'll go to old Rome. Agreed?"

Crown leans down to Sirius and looks him deep in the eyes.

"Do you want to go to the circus?"

Sirius wags his tail.

"Right then," smirks Warner. "Good decision. I'll add on another hundred dollars a week. For the Clark Gable of the dog world."

"When do we start?" asks Crown.

"Immediately," says Warner. "After all, the new star of the circus ring stills need to figure out what his performance is going to be."

*

Sarasota is a small backwater in southern Florida. The only reason it's on the map at all is because the headquarters of Ringling Bros. and Barnum & Bailey is here.

Crown has accompanied Sirius on the long, cross-country journey so that they have time to say good-bye to each other. It is hard for him to watch as the little dog walks away, glancing back one last time before disappearing into the big tent.

So Sirius is now a circus dog.

He lives in the "village." That's the name for the meadow behind the tent where the artists' trailers are parked. Four-legged artists usually live in the "zoo." That's what they call the adjoining meadow with the stalls, enclosures and cages. Gargantua lives here too, in a special cage, of course. It's made of bulletproof glass, has air-conditioning, and is pulled by six grays when it needs to be transported to the tent.

But Sirius lives in the village, because he's primarily involved with the two-legged artists. Starting with the planned opening number: Hercules will compete against "Drago, the world's strongest man," whose signature stunt is supporting his own mountain of muscles on a single-finger handstand.

Before the break, the great magician Manzini will present his famous time machine, which is to make Hercules smaller and smaller until—eventually—he goes from being a young pup in Manzini's hand to evaporating into thin air.

The highlight will be the final stunt. Barbarossa, the legendary lion tamer—who lost his right hand after Benares the lion almost mauled him to death—will have Hercules ride on Benares's back. For the first time in the history of the animal kingdom, a terrier and a lion will confront each other.

That's the plan, at least. Now they just have to make it work.

Sirius shares a trailer with Manzini. Primarily because no one else is allowed to discover the secret behind the time machine, which is also in the trailer, covered with a black cloth. Manzini is so secretive that he even keeps the curtains closed.

Barbarossa doesn't need a trailer. He sleeps with the beasts of prey. He sometimes has straw in his hair in the mornings, and even smells like a lion.

Drago can be recognized by the fact that he gets around solely by walking on his hands. To him, this seems completely normal. When someone is talking with him, his knees are at eye level, and his head answers from below, upside down. Conversations with him are always interesting, in any case.

What a wonderful village, thinks Sirius to himself. There can't be any other village in existence with this many things to see. Where else could you see a Lilliputian cheerfully greet five Chinese women who are juggling tea cups on a unicycle, while nearby a man chains his wife to a spinning wheel and throws knives at her?

The man, by the way, is the infamous "El Diablo," who made headlines when he threw a dagger straight into his first wife's heart. He was completely drunk during the performance, and therefore not criminally responsible.

And Sirius hasn't met everyone in the village yet, not even close. The Lilliputian, for example, is alleged to speak eighty-four languages, even Irku, a language which is only spoken in the southern Antarctic. The Lilliputian was put to the test when a tightrope walker arrived from this very region; he had an acrobatic penguin in the program. And he confirmed it: the Lilliputian speaks fluent Irku.

* * *

Manzini doesn't speak at all. He cloaks himself in silence. Presumably because he fears that some unguarded word might slip out, enabling people to decipher the secret of his time machine.

Each evening, he sits on his bed and listens to the same radio station. Food is brought to him from the canteen, and he silently puts it onto two plates in order to share with Sirius. Later, he nods politely to Sirius, which is intended to mean *good night*, and turns out the light.

Strangely, he talks in his sleep. But as soon as he utters the words "*macchina del tempo*," he awakes with a start and shines the beam of his flashlight around the room. Then he goes back to sleep.

What could the secret be, wonders Sirius?

*

A magician can rehearse anywhere, but a lion tamer needs the circus tent. As does an acrobat. One person's wild animal cage in the circus ring is another's trapeze under the dome of the Big Top.

Barbarossa is going "big-topping" today. That's how he puts it to Sirius. He grins and rips his shirt from his body as he heads off. "Lions hate shirts," he says. His naked torso resembles a battlefield. It gives a good indication of just how many times the paws have already caught him. A scar runs diagonally across his back and, of all places, right through the middle of the tattooed lion's head between his shoulder blades.

He had "Krone" tattooed on the hand he lost. The Krone Circus was where Barbarossa started out.

Benares is already waiting inside his cage in the circus ring. He circles nervously, impatiently, close to the bars. He is a fine specimen of a wild cat. Every movement he makes exudes unbridled strength.

The lion snarls as he catches sight of the dog.

"That means 'hello,'" translates Barbarossa.

Sirius doesn't want to know what it sounds like when Benares is saying "adieu."

Benares rises up on his haunches to his full height to greet Barbarossa. He towers over him by at least a yard.

Sirius is trembling all over.

This doesn't escape Barbarossa's attention, so he says: "You don't need to be afraid. He's not hungry anymore."

To be on the safe side, the keeper throws another small animal carcass into the cage, which Benares promptly devours in one go.

"Come on, we're going in," says Barbarossa, picking Sirius up and opening the cage door.

Benares skulks at the other end of the cage. He snorts as his nose picks up the scent.

"This is Hercules," says Barbarossa by way of introduction. To Sirius, he whispers softly: "Always wait for *him* to come to you. Never approach him. Otherwise he'll defend his territory."

The lion tamer goes on to offer more advice: "It's best to ignore him. Then he'll ignore you too."

It's not easy to ignore a lion. And it's especially hard for small dogs to do so.

Sirius sees Benares slowly approaching him, coming closer and closer, until the head and mighty mane are so close in front of his eyes that warm breath blows into his face.

The lion sniffs at the dog, then turns around and lies down lethargically in the sand of the circus ring.

"He has accepted you," says Barbarossa. "You are now in his pride."

Is there any greater relief than being accepted into a lion's pride?

But Sirius soon puts the good experience into perspective when he—back outside the bars again—follows what happens next in the cage. Barbarossa straps a stuffed toy animal onto the lion's back in order to lead him a step further toward the intended performance. But without success; Benares rolls angrily back and forth on the floor, shakes off the rider and tears it to shreds.

The lion tamer persists, refusing to give up.

Later, the circus tent belongs to the acrobats. Sirius watches the "Flying Turbans." Eight Indians swing toward one another at a dizzying height on the trapeze, and at the moment of flying interchange they each execute a triple somersault. It's not yet going entirely without a glitch. Sometimes one of the Indians ends up reaching into nothingness, sometimes two crash their heads together.

* * *

Then comes "Don Dente." The man's reputation precedes him like a clap of thunder. He can take a gondola containing four members of the audience and pull it up to the Big Top dome with his teeth.

Today he is rehearsing the climax of his performance: with his arms tied behind his back and his eyes blindfolded, Don Dente strides across the high wire, somersaults into the air in a high arc, misses the landing with his feet, goes into free fall—then bites onto the rope and hangs there by his teeth.

Sirius wants to clap. For the first time in his life, he understands the humans' compulsion for clapping their hands together loudly. It just doesn't work with paws.

*

Sirius is always relieved to find Drago standing outside his door in the morning instead of the lion tamer. Training with him is fun, just like playing.

The number is a show fight between Hercules, the fearless dog from the eponymous Hollywood film, and Drago, "the world's strongest man."

When it comes to this kind of act, Hercules has an ace up his sleeve (as the saying goes, even though the individual in question doesn't actually have sleeves). Being the audience's darling is his thing. All he needs to do is act strong.

Drago, on the other hand, really *is* strong. And he looks even stronger when he's not walking on his hands, but instead standing firmly with both feet on the floor. A muscle behemoth with a small, shaven head protruding out.

* * *

"How about . . ." suggests Drago, "if you were to push me with your paw, and I fall over?"

Hearing the audience's roar of laughter in his mind, he can't help but laugh out loud himself. Then his expression becomes serious all of a sudden, and he thinks for a moment. He gazes vacantly into space, his mouth wide open. He remembers that he is supposed to be the "world's strongest man." So why would he fall over?

"Or how about," he suggests, "you nudge me with your paw, then I fling you into the audience as hard as I can?"

But even that doesn't seem to convince him. Once again, he stares open-mouthed into nothingness. Fling a sweet little dog into the audience? That's just not the done thing.

So, be nice and still demonstrate strength. That's the trick.

"How about," suggests Drago, "if you nudge me with your paw, and I do three or four somersaults backward then land in a one-handed handstand?"

Now the acrobat in him has been awakened.

"And then you jump up on me, sit on my feet and press me down to the floor?"

Sirius wags his tail. They try it out at once. The five Chinese women on the unicycle ride past, giggle and raise five thumbs up in the air in approval.

More and more ideas are coming to Drago now. How about if he were to do a headstand on Hercules's head? They would just need to make a little support as reinforcement, cover it with correctly colored fur and put it out of sight beneath the dog.

Now the illusionist in Drago is awakening. Sirius is curious to see what else will awaken in the mountain of muscle.

By now, Sirius has also met the Lilliputian. His name is Terry and he has been with Ringling Bros. for almost twenty years. Sirius is curious to find out how it came to be that he speaks eighty-four languages.

It seems that Terry can also read minds, for he replies: "I could already speak thirty-seven languages when I was born. Maybe nature knows that a dwarf will need to travel a lot until he finds his place in the world."

They take a walk together through the zoo. Terry knows every animal. And there are two thousand animals living there.

"That's Moyo the elephant," he explains. "A few years ago, Moyo stopped in the middle of his act and ran over to a little girl in the audience. He touched the girl with his trunk, right here."

Terry points at his heart.

"Moyo made a sound, like this."

Terry imitates the doleful sound of a saxophone.

"The parents took the girl to the hospital at once. As it turns out, she was suffering from an acute heart defect. Moyo saved her life."

Sirius is impressed.

They pause next to a moose.

"This is Plutarch," says Terry sadly. "He used to be able to dance the tango. A professor from Vienna taught him. The professor died one day at 3:21 precisely." Terry looks at

Sirius. "Plutarch has dementia now, so it's been a long time since he's been able to dance the tango. But every day, at exactly 3:21, he has tears in his eyes."

Sirius can barely believe it.

"And yet he doesn't have a watch," adds Terry.

In front of the lion cage, they stop. Benares seems to be pleased to see Sirius again. He purrs and wags his tail tassel.

"Crazy story," says Terry. "Benares has never gotten over the fact that he bit off Barbarossa's hand that time in the Krone Circus. It's the reason why he left Germany. The Hitler salute, all those outstretched hands surrounding him incessantly. It always reminded him of the incident. Hands make him feel guilty."

Every animal has his story. The zoo is the biggest history book of the animal kingdom, and the Lilliputian is flicking through it.

Suddenly the Lilliputian asks: "What's your story, by the way?"

Sirius doesn't know where to start.

The Lilliputian nods: "Sometimes the end tells you everything you need to know about the beginning."

Both of them reflect on how long they had to travel in order to find their place in the world.

Sirius feels happy.

*

Today, Manzini will talk.

The day has come for him to reveal his secret. Otherwise his time machine won't work.

Sirius is almost bursting with curiosity.

Manzini draws the curtains in the trailer. Ceremoniously, he unveils the specter that has been standing in their room for weeks, and addresses Sirius for the first time ever: "This is my time machine."

All Sirius sees is a black box.

"There's a hole here," says Manzini. "That's where you'll slip in."

Sirius looks at him expectantly.

"And that's it," says Manzini, bringing his explanation to a close. "There's nothing else you need to know."

He lays the cloth back over the box.

That's it? Sirius doesn't understand.

"That's it," repeats Manzini. "I'll take care of everything else."

He takes his coat from the wardrobe, puts on his hat and goes.

*

World history is treating Jack Warner well.

Hirohito, the Emperor of Japan, has sunk the U.S. Pacific Fleet in Pearl Harbor. Yesterday, Hitler declared war on the United States of America. And today, just one day later, Jack

Warner has in his hands a stage play which works perfectly with the political background.

Its name is *Everybody Comes to Rick's*. Warner immediately gives the green light for filming. And he already has a better title in mind: *Casablanca*.

The movie is crying out for Humphrey Bogart. Only he can play Rick.

"All it needs now is a little more heart," thinks Warner. "How about if Rick were to have a dog? Hercules, for example?"

That would make the final scene more touching too. "We'll always have Hercules," Humphrey Bogart would say. Instead of Paris.

Jack Warner hates Paris.

He can picture it already, Bogey standing there with the dog under his arm on the airfield, saying to Ilsa: "Here's looking at Hercules, kid."

"That would work too," says Bogey, shrugging his shoulders.

But the plan is doomed to fail. Hercules is not available. It's December, and he's about to make his debut in the circus. After that, he goes on tour.

"Fine," sighs Warner. "Then I guess you'll have to have Paris after all."

December will be a fateful month for all concerned this year. But they have no idea what lies ahead.

Hitler has no idea of what awaits his army in Russia. Contrary to his hopes, he won't have Stalingrad.

Rick has no idea that, in the end, he won't just have Paris, but the beginning of a wonderful friendship too.

And Sirius? If only he knew . . .

Carl and Rahel set off to Sarasota. They want to be there, of course, when Hercules conquers the Big Top.

Tomorrow is the day. The day The Greatest Show on Earth kicks off. The tickets have been sold out for weeks.

The dress rehearsal has already taken place. By now, Hercules can ride Benares and fight with Drago, and the time machine is working too.

The tent is decorated for Christmas, which seems particularly strange in Sarasota because it feels like summer right now. It's bathing suit season by the sea.

It's very unlikely that Bing Crosby's dream of a white Christmas will be fulfilled. But his new song is still pretty catchy. It plays constantly on Manzini's little radio. Sirius can't think about that now. He is too agitated. Manzini is agitated too.

"It's called stage fright," explains Drago.

He lights up a cigarette and smokes it from the corner of his mouth while balancing upside down on both hands. It makes him cough. Nature has done a good job: walking upright has its advantages, at least for smokers.

Barbarossa is sleeping. Nothing calms the nerves more than a nap in the lion's cage; that's his motto. He slumbers peacefully, his head rising and falling in time with Benares's mighty chest.

* * *

Next door is Gargantua's cage. The huge black beast stares vacantly into the distance. When Sirius appears, his eyes twinkle.

"Do you see his smile?" asks the keeper.

Sirius sees it. As scary a sight as the gorilla is, he really is smiling.

"Crazy, right?" says the keeper. "When Gargantua was captured in Africa, a hunter sprayed acid in his face. Since then, his face has been frozen, and he always looks as though he's smiling."

Or perhaps he really is smiling? Who knows?

*

The premiere.

Nine thousand people stream into the tent, two of whom are Carl and Rahel, and the excitement in the fully packed rows is bubbling even before the orchestra begins its opening fanfare.

Sirius peeps through the curtain, but he can't make out any familiar faces in the excited mass. Never has he seen such a crowd of people, not even at the harbor in Genoa when the *Conte di Savoia* set sail. The tent, too, seems more vast to him than the ocean.

Well, it is The Greatest Show on Earth, after all.

The lights go out and the circus director steps into the spotlight. He greets the audience with utter conviction that all their expectations for the evening, however high they are, will be exceeded by far, and culminates with the words: "Introducing Hercules, in his battle against Drago, the world's strongest man!"

Fanfare from the orchestra.

Hercules strides into the arena, accompanied by the sounds of a triumphal march reserved solely for fearless gladiators.

Rahel is so moved that she has to blow her nose.

Then Drago appears. The muscle mountain is oiled and glistens in the spotlight like antique marble.

The audience quickly sides with Hercules, of course, cheering him on and rejoicing when he lets the oily warrior have it.

They also applaud rapturously the acrobatic feats with which Drago frees himself again and again from seemingly hopeless situations.

The dramatic duel reaches its climax when Drago goes into a handstand on Hercules's head, towers up and, almost unbelievably, ends up balancing on just one single finger.

The audience goes wild.

Next come fire-eaters, elephant pyramids, flying turbans, dancing hyenas and so on. Everything is top-notch. But Carl and Rahel are like proud parents, waiting for their child to be in the spotlight again. Even El Diablo only wins their partial attention.

*　*　*

Fanfare from the orchestra.

The circus director announces the famous magician Manzini and his time machine, which will now transport Sirius back to his childhood in front of the audience's eyes.

Manzini, suddenly becoming unusually talkative here in the tent, asks Hercules loud and clear whether he is aware of the mortal danger involved in this extraordinary experiment.

Hercules nods bravely.

Without further ado, Manzini unveils the time machine.

It's nothing but a black box on a small pedestal, barely any bigger than the dog. Unfathomably, it seems to be hovering in the air.

The magician says good-bye to Hercules in the way someone might before a long journey, and the dog slips into the time machine.

Rapt silence in the tent.

Manzini conjures the time machine to set back the clock of life. He says a magic word—and look! Out of the time machine jumps Hercules, except half the size he was before.

A gasp of disbelief ripples through the audience.

The same performance again. Little Hercules slips into the time machine. Magic word—and look! Out slips Hercules, except even smaller.

"Do you want to see how Hercules looked when he first came into the world?" Manzini asks the audience.

They are speechless, experiencing a wonder that quashes all the laws of nature.

So he continues regardless. The tiny little creature creeps into the time machine. Magic word—and look! Out scrabbles Hercules as a whelp.

Manzini holds him up high, and with a flourish of his hand—magic word and hey presto!—Hercules vanishes into thin air.

And the time machine? Manzini dismantles the little black box—empty.

The magician bows to thunderous applause.

"For the love of God," whispers Rahel. "Where's Sirius?"

"I don't know," Carl whispers back. He's spellbound too.

And the show goes on. One sensation after the next. Gargantua in his cage. Don Dente and his bite into the tightrope. The polar bears' double somersaults. The five Chinese women on the unicycle. But Carl and Rahel aren't concerned by whether the artistes accomplish their feats. They're whispering to each other, wondering where their dog might be.

There he is! Hercules trots into the tent, clearly exhausted from all the time traveling. The relieved audience welcomes him with a standing ovation.

The circus director greets present-day Hercules and wishes him luck with his next task.

Fanfare from the orchestra.

"Viewers of a nervous disposition," he warns, "should leave the tent now. As should viewers with heart problems.

Hercules is now going to confront Benares, Africa's fiercest lion!"

The audience is almost at the breaking point. Most of the onlookers reach gratefully for the masks with eye slits that are being passed around the rows. Some faint.

Benares lurks in his cage, grunting with relish in anticipation of the dog which is about to be thrown for him to devour. Barbarossa is using all of his force to hold him back.

Then Hercules steps through the cage door. It's a small step for the dog, but a big step for the animal world. For the first time in the history of the animal kingdom, a fox terrier is standing opposite a lion.

Unbelievably, the dog jumps bravely onto the King of the Mammals and rides him triumphantly around the circus ring.

The audience goes wild.

Rahel holds her hands in front of the eye slits of her mask and sighs: "Is he still alive?"

"He's alive," says Carl.

*

All of America is eager to see Hercules. The final performance in Sarasota takes place on New Year's Eve, then the circus takes down the tent and goes on tour.

An undertaking which is much easier said than done.

Even the departure of the average four-person family on a journey isn't without a certain amount of commotion. So naturally the decampment of a 1,500-strong circus troop with 2,000 animals in tow is a gargantuan task in comparison. Not to mention dismantling the circus tent itself.

A chartered train is waiting at the platform in Sarasota. Wagon after wagon is being loaded up. By the end, the train is a mile long.

The traveling village and zoo-on-wheels, a gorilla and Hercules in the thick of it all, sets off on a cross-country journey.

President Roosevelt himself has granted the touring circus special dispensation. Rail transport is strictly limited during wartime, but the circus is classified as being "essential for the nation's morale."

Only now does it become completely clear why the spectacle is regarded as The Greatest Show on Earth.

Four million visitors are expected during the course of the tour. The first stop is Cleveland.

Manzini has driven on ahead in his own car. Through fear that something might happen to his precious time machine on the train.

At their destination, he and Hercules share a trailer again. Everything is just the same as always.

Except that it isn't.

Hercules seems agitated. He eyes the covered time machine nervously and growls. Strange. After all, he's very familiar with it by now.

When Drago appears, the dog flinches back and lowers his tail close to his body.

"Bizarre," says Drago.

He launches into a stunt in which Hercules always obeys by jumping onto his back, but the dog just stares into nothingness.

Barbarossa, who they call over at once, is equally baffled.

"Hercules, come here!" he calls, stretching out his hand. The dog doesn't react.

"It's like he's a completely different dog!" gapes Drago.

Manzini wrinkles his forehead thoughtfully. "The Turk," he mumbles.

*

News of the puzzling incident does the rounds in next to no time. John Ringling North himself comes storming over.

"What's this I'm hearing?" he roars. "Hercules isn't Hercules?"

Barbarossa, Drago and Manzini stand there in confusion. Even Hercules, who it seems isn't Hercules, looks confused.

"What's going on here?" explodes John Ringling North. "I demand to know at once what's going on!"

"We don't know, either," says Drago timidly.

Barbarossa can only stammer. "The dog doesn't recognize us anymore. It's like he's completely different."

"Hercules!" Barbarossa commands the dog. The dog doesn't react, he simply whimpers helplessly.

"See," says Drago with a shrug of his shoulders. "It's a mystery."

* * *

John Ringling North does see. He sees with the eyes of a circus director whose star act has just vanished into thin air right in front of him.

"This is a catastrophe," he laments. "A catastrophe."

Manzini has only one explanation: "The time machine."

"Oh, give it a rest!" bellows the circus director. "Hercules didn't *really* evaporate into thin air, or do you actually believe that?"

Manzini isn't a fantasist. He's an illusionist. And the two are worlds apart. This is a matter of professional honor.

But here he stands, and he has no other option. He has to reveal the secret of his time machine. For years he has protected it, concealed it, guarded it, shielded it, silenced it. And now he has to reveal it.

So what appears to be one dog is in truth four dogs. Four dogs of different sizes. As soon as the smaller one slips into the time machine, the bigger one disappears. How exactly that happens is something that Manzini will continue to keep under wraps.

All he says is this: "After the last performance, the dogs were switched."

"Switched?" asks the circus director in horror.

"Well, puppies grow bigger, after all," explains Manzini. "In three months the puppy won't be a puppy anymore, and the medium-size dog will be as big as Hercules."

This sheds some light on things. The dogs were switched for the tour. The circus director thinks intensely.

"Who switched the dogs?" he asks.

"The Turk," replies Manzini. "He's an animal handler of sorts. He brings us magicians the animals we need—rabbits, doves and so on. He also takes away with him the animals that we don't need anymore."

The mystery is solved. In his haste, the Turk confused the dogs and took Hercules with him by mistake.

"This is your fault!" declares the circus director, prodding his index finger into Manzini's chest. "If you had been paying attention, the mix-up would never have happened. Tell the Turk to bring Hercules back at once!"

With those words, he considers the matter dealt with. He strides off assertively.

The dog who isn't Hercules didn't understand a single word. Drago, if he is honest, didn't, either.

Barbarossa can only hope that Manzini knows how to sort things out. He is a magician, after all.

But for once, Manzini can't conjure up what they need.

The Turk was there just a week ago, and he won't be back again for three months. No one knows exactly where he goes in between. It seems as though he, too, has vanished into thin air.

*

The Turk has long since boarded a ship to Europe. He has already sold the puppies on board. An old lady was completely ecstatic with her purchase.

She wanted to have one of the trained rabbits too, but he needs to take these to the Sarassani Circus in Dresden. Along with the talking parrot. The four dancing cats are expected in the Pirelli Circus in Rome.

Arriving on dry land, in Bremen, the Turk gets rid of one of the two remaining dogs. The smaller one. Bartered for his hotel bill.

Now he just has the bigger dog in his possession. He should have thrown him overboard, he thinks to himself. Who would want some shaggy mongrel that's been discharged from the circus?

On his next stop, the Turk simply opens the car door and pushes the dog out in the middle of the city.

Sirius lies there in the gutter. He feels dizzy. At first he thought the journey was part of the tour they were always talking about. But no, this is obviously not Cleveland.

Sirius rubs his eyes. Thick snow is falling from the sky. For some reason, his surroundings look familiar. Is he in Berlin? If he's not mistaken, then that must be the Kurfürstendamm up ahead.

And it is.

Could it be possible that Manzini's time machine really worked?

Before he can give the matter any more thought, Sirius finds himself standing in front of his tree.

"You're here?" asks the tree.

"Yes," says Sirius, exhausted.

"How?" asks the tree.

"Oh, it's a long story," sighs Sirius.

Isn't that Frau Zinke? She's sweeping the snow from the pavement, just like she used to.

An SS man comes their way. Frau Zinke salutes: "*Heil Hitler, Herr Hauptsturmführer!*"

"Is this *your* dog?" asks the Hauptsturmführer.

"Which dog?" asks Frau Zinke.

"This one here," says the Hauptsturmführer, leaning over to Sirius and stroking him. "Good boy."

Frau Zinke pauses. "No, but for some reason he looks familiar."

She wrinkles her brow and thinks back.

"There was a dog here once, many years ago, that looked similar to this one. He was called Levi, if I remember rightly."

"Levi?" laughs the Hauptsturmführer. "The kind of people who gave their dogs names like that aren't around anymore."

"That's true," giggles Frau Zinke. "I'm getting old and forgetful."

The SS man clicks his heels. "Then he's a stray. Impounded!"

He leads Sirius away.

"Look what I've brought you," calls the Hauptsturmführer as he arrives home to his family that evening. "Our new dog. Hansi."

PART 3

REICHSMARSCHALL HERMANN GÖRING has many roles; among other titles he is also the Reich Minister for the Conservation of Forests. The Reich Ministry for the Conservation of Forests, in turn, is in command of the Reich Ministry for Nature Conservation, and within this authority is the Department for Bird Protection.

One might think that the well-being of blackbirds, thrushes, finches and starlings would be a low priority during wartime—but that's not the case. The Führer is a self-proclaimed bird lover. There's hardly anything that lies closer to his heart than the fluttering creatures. He has personally vowed to "hold his protective hand over the hedges."

What hedges? After all, birds fly. But the Führer has already thought of that. His protective hand even stretches to the hedges that have only recently been conquered. Hedges in Russia, for example.

The soldiers on the front have been instructed to show consideration for the birds while creating new "living space." They receive guidelines on the construction of nesting boxes and feeders. Tons of hemp seed and sunflower seeds are transported to the front, as winter sustenance for the birds.

This is the kind of thing that usually gets forgotten, but in this war, the birds are being looked after.

Erwin Wünsche is the man who takes care of all this. He is the leader of the Department for Bird Protection. Office 322, Floor 2. And he's good at what he does. He was recently promoted to Hauptsturmführer by his highest superior.

"The bird," said Göring in his address, "is our ambassador. We Germans are a people of the forests. Unlike the Jews. They are a people of the desert. German forests and German birds, they belong together. A bird singing in the forest is the most beautiful German song in existence." Wünsche was deeply moved by these words.

Since then, whenever he hears a blackbird or thrush singing its song, he clicks his heels together and cries, *"Heil, Hitler!"*

Wünsche was dead set on getting himself a German shepherd. German man and German dog, they belong together too.

But Heinrich Docht, in Office 321 next door, advised him against it. His two-year-old daughter was attacked by his German shepherd, and now she only has one eye.

Wünsche's children are older, admittedly: Rudi has just become a member of the Hitler Youth's Jungvolk, and Ulrich is already a patrol leader. But still. They need to embark on their journey through life with two eyes, that's the very least the Jungvolk should be able to expect.

And so it came about that a fox terrier joined their household: Hansi.

The Hauptsturmführer is no longer that bothered about the breed, as long as it's a dog. With humans, of course, it's a different matter. Humans are not all equal—oh no, in that context race is very important.

He even goes a step further: any dog called Hansi has to be a German dog.

Mistakes can be made, however. When it comes to Sirius, Erwin Wünsche has made the wrong choice. But how could he possibly know that?

"Hansi!" he commands. "Walkies!"

A walk wouldn't be the right description for what the two of them are doing. The Hauptsturmführer marches in goose-step through the streets, with Sirius following on a taut lead. They both like lingering around trees; the dog certainly does, and the master even more so. It makes Wünsche feel like a proud representative of the People of the Forest.

Here and there, the Hauptsturmführer addresses a passerby who doesn't seem Germanic enough to him.

"You there!" he calls. "Come here a moment!"

The passerby then has to show his papers. After all, he could be one of those desert people still trespassing through the undergrowth of the German forests.

"Strange birds" is what the Hauptsturmführer calls such people. The German Reich needs to be protected from them. Bird Protection includes this too.

Unbelievable that this man, of all people, now has a Jewish dog at the end of his lead.

*   *   *

The dog still clearly remembers the day when Father Lilien-cron said: "It's dangerous out there if you have a Jewish name. We'll find a beautiful new name for you. Then you can give the Aryans the runaround."

And so Levi became Sirius.

Now the danger is even greater. Sirius is living in the lair of a Hauptsturmführer who has pledged his allegiance to the swastika of the master race.

One needs to be called Hansi to survive in a place like that.

*

The Wünsches live in a house on Bülowstraße, not far from Kleistpark, where the office of the Reich Ministry for Nature Conservation is located. So Erwin Wünsche only has a short commute, and often comes home for lunch.

Their town house isn't bad for an official of the Department for Bird Protection. The Traube family, the former owners of the Traube screw factory, certainly used to feel at home here. That is until their property was Aryanized, and the Traubes deported.

One of the property's most impressive features is the garden. And it's so much more than a garden; more like a large market garden. Vegetable beds, herb beds, flower beds, fruit trees, greenhouses. The Wünsche family feeds itself from its own soil.

Grapes are the only thing they don't have. Not one single grape. That would be too disrespectful. Other than that, everything that the German soil can produce grows here.

"Your tomatoes are the best," Göring once said. One tomato even made its way to the Führer, and he was allegedly very impressed by it. The Führer is completely uncompromising when it comes to tomatoes. If there's something he can judge, then it's tomatoes. After all, he himself predominantly eats organic food.

Cooking is a woman's business. That's why, in the garden and the kitchen, Erwin Wünsche's wife, Gertrud, commands the regiment. She has a sturdy, rugged figure, perfectly suited for garden work. In fact, whenever she lays down the spade or hoe she looks strangely incomplete.

People whose daily work takes place in the plant kingdom tend to enjoy talking about it, but seldom reap any interest. It is the same for Gertrud.

"The caterpillars are at the savoy cabbage again," she complains.

"Are they?" replies Erwin, elsewhere in his thoughts.

"The radishes are already coming up," says Gertrud cheerfully.

"Good," says Erwin.

What else can one say in response to that? Erwin has other problems. The Final Solution to the Jewish Question is a done deal. Eleven million Jews from all over Europe are on the death lists. The first trains to the Auschwitz extermination camp are already setting off. How can it all be made to go smoothly?

"Gassing. Will it really work?" asks Erwin.

"No idea," says Gertrud.

"Eleven million of them!" cries Erwin.

"Uh-huh," responds Gertrud briefly.

She simply isn't interested in his work-related problems. And as it happens, the Final Solution isn't Wünsche's problem either. He works in the Department for Bird Protection. But all the authorities are closely interconnected, and career progression can be an unpredictable thing.

Take Dr. Manfred Gürtel, for example. He is Wünsche's direct superior in the Reich Ministry of Forests. Gürtel will soon be transferred to the Reich Main Security Office to lead Department 211 of Chartered Trains. People with good organizational skills are in demand right now.

Erwin Wünsche has good organizational skills. Recently Göring ordered five thousand nesting boxes for Carinhall, his hunting estate in the Schorfheide forest. It takes a lot of wood to make five thousand nesting boxes. And Göring's order was: "On the double!" Wünsche mastered the task. Might he possibly become Gürtel's successor? Why didn't they take *him* instead of Gürtel?

These are the questions that are worrying him. It's hard for a Hauptsturmführer to switch off at the end of the working day. One seldom sees him sitting in the armchair; instead, he tends to pace up and down the living room, nervous, silent, lost in thought. Five thousand nest boxes, Department 211, Gürtel, on the double.

The children loiter around, bored. They wear their Hitler Youth uniforms even at home.

"Play with Hansi!" calls their mother.

The children look at each other, clueless. They don't really know what to do with Hansi. Ulrich, the patrol leader, throws the dog his swastika armband and calls "Catch!"

Sirius flinches. This is supposed to be fun?

Rudi, the Jungvolk newbie, picks up a cushion and presses it down onto the dog's head.

"You're dead!" he cries.

Sirius yelps and scampers away.

"Hansi can't play," complain the children. "He's stupid."

"Then find something respectable to read," says their mother. "Read the *Stürmer.*"

Ulrich and Rudi fetch the flashlight instead, then go into the garden and hunt for snails, which they jeeringly hack to pieces with a spade.

The Volksempfänger radio broadcasts the request show for the Wehrmacht. Magda Hain sings "Seagull, You're Flying Home." Sirius feels sad. Oh, how he would love to be that seagull right now.

Before going to bed each evening, Gertrud polishes her husband's boots back to a high shine. At night, the boots Sirius has been afraid of his entire life stand right next to his basket. What a nightmare.

Moonlight falls through the window. The Big Dog is in the starry sky, and he's worried. After all, he can see how much the little dog is suffering. Sirius is afraid that they've long forgotten him on the other side of the world.

*

Forgotten him? Not in the slightest! John Ringling North, the circus director, has alerted the Crowns about what happened, the Crowns went straight to Jack Warner, Jack Warner even asked the president of the United States for help, and Roosevelt in turn immediately sent diplomatic cables to all the U.S. ambassadors. All in vain.

But how could they hope to be successful? The dog has disappeared without a trace, he could be anywhere in the world. Or, in the worst case scenario, no longer in the world at all.

Rahel is in floods of tears, inconsolable in her grief.

Carl stares into the distance, horror-stricken. Sirius was his life. Without his dog, there is no reason to get up in the morning.

The circus director is beside himself. The Greatest Show on Earth stands or falls by Hercules. His name is in block capitals on all the posters.

He is on top of the bill.

Jack Warner is cursing. Who will rescue old Rome now? And Hollywood without Hercules? Unthinkable.

Not to mention the hearts of the nation. Hercules has won over an audience of millions. What if the people find out that their sweetheart has disappeared without a trace?

An absolute catastrophe.

* * *

Jack Warner calls for absolute silence on the matter. After all, there's still hope. Soon the Turk will be back. He is the only one who knows where Sirius ended up.

Sirius—each of them now suddenly realize—changed all of their lives. He is their fate.

And yet all he wanted to do was play. He played into the hearts of the people, even when he was still called Levi and receiving two nut triangles for a performance. Then he transformed himself into Sirius, and his star rose in Hollywood. Hercules was his greatest role, and he was even in The Greatest Show on Earth.

A small dog, but such a great transformation artist. No one knows who he *really* is.

"He was always fleeing from something," says Carl sadly. "Perhaps this time he really managed it."

"Don't say that!" protests Rahel, bursting into tears again.

Secretly, even she fears that they will never see Sirius again. Where could he be? Long gone across the mountains? Somewhere on the ocean? Or on land, together with other dogs. Happy. The most important thing is that he's happy.

The Turk returns.

He turns up on the doorstep one day, not suspecting a thing. He has three fox terriers with him, of differing sizes, as agreed.

Manzini rushes toward him.

"Where's Hercules?" he shouts, before going on to explain what happened.

The Turk goes pale with shock. He stammers his story, aware that he is unleashing even greater unhappiness with every word.

Carl and Rahel listen breathlessly.

As soon as the story reaches German soil, they all shudder.

"Germany?" calls Carl in disbelief.

The Turk suspects that the news of where the story ends will be equally disquieting: Berlin.

"Berlin?" shrieks Rahel.

Yes, that's how life plays out. Sirius isn't just playing with life; life is playing with Sirius too. That's the magic we call fate.

Manzini knows this. He smiles and thinks to himself that, in a way, his time machine did work after all.

Sirius is back where he came from. He has saved everyone, the Liliencrons, the settlers in Luckyville, the princess on the South Pacific island of "Hula"—and now he himself needs to be saved.

He desperately needs a guardian angel.

And there happens to be one in his very own family. But Jewish guardian angels don't have permission to land in Berlin.

*

The days in the Wünsche household drag by slowly. They begin with the Hauptsturmführer marching off to the office,

then the children trot off to school—and from then on Sirius
is alone, for Gertrud disappears off into her vegetable beds.

She crawls through the lettuce, she scrabbles through the
turnips, she weeds and plucks. Her head is hard to make out
amid all the heads of cabbage. Now and then she sits up,
stretches her crooked back and groans.

She has tried to make use of Hansi for the garden work, in the
area of snail extermination, for example, but he's useless. He
is repulsed by snails. And by Gertrud too. Her rustic features,
the crude clothing, the chapped hands, everything is a horror
to him. The hobgoblin with the apron just doesn't fit into his
idea of what a woman should be. Impossible to believe that
she is of the same gender as Gloria Hayson, Carole Lombard
and Rahel.

The clock hands creep toward midday. The house begins to
smell of stew, sometimes with peas, sometimes with potatoes.

The Hauptsturmführer has to swallow whatever Gertrud
has brewed up for him. The dish also dictates the topics of
conversation.

"Peas are very healthy," says Gertrud.

"And green," comments her husband.

"Potatoes," says Gertrud with contentment.

"German potatoes," corrects her husband.

Ulrich and Rudi sit there silently at the table. They try to
follow the adults' conversation.

Once the last pea has been chewed, the Hauptsturmführer
gets up, clicks his heels together and goes back to the office.

* * *

Now the afternoon stretches before Sirius; a seemingly endless lowland of boredom with only the odd small crest to awake his interest.

Sometimes the postman rings the doorbell. Sometimes the wind slams a window shut. Sometimes the kettle whistles on the stove. But nothing more than that.

The children obediently do their homework.

"Name Kriemhild's three brothers in the *Song of the Nibelungs*," murmurs Ulrich.

"Gunther, Gernot and Giselher," calls Rudi proudly.

Good to know.

Ulrich claps the book shut. He wants to play now instead.

"Hansi," he calls, waking the dog, "come on, we're going Jew-hunting!"

The dog doesn't know the game. Nor does it sound like one he would like to know. But the children tug him out onto the street regardless.

"Here," says Ulrich, the patrol leader, holding a scrap of material under Hansi's nose. "This is what Jews smell like."

The material comes from a coat that the Gestapo ripped from an old man's body the day before. Ulrich happened to walk past just as the man was seized. He picked up the coat and tore off the breast pocket with the Jewish star.

The dog is now expected to pick up the trail. The children spur him on. They chase him into dark doorways, up flights of stairs, and before every apartment door they call excitedly: "Can you smell them?"

Sirius pretends to be sniffing around. After all, he doesn't want to be a spoilsport. The children wait eagerly for the fruits of his tracking instinct.

Nothing, again.

He could, of course, play with fire and occasionally act as though he's on the right track. The children would be delighted. They would praise him and pamper him.

But that wasn't an option. The children could then batter at the door, and perhaps they really would find what they were looking for. Then Sirius would be a snitch. That's what people call Jews who betray their own people in order to rescue themselves.

No, Sirius would rather be a failure than risk that. Rudi kicks him in disappointment.

"Hansi is stupid," announces Ulrich that evening to his father. A report of their failed hunt follows.

The father reminds them that it wasn't the easiest of tasks. Of the 160,000 Berlin Jews, he estimates, only 15,000 remain. Hidden all over the city. In cellars, in attics, in back rooms.

"So it's entirely possible that you'll often come away empty-handed."

"He won't hunt for snails, either," says Gertrud sadly.

"Maybe he's just not a hunting dog," suggests Rudi.

"A German dog that isn't a hunting dog?" exclaims the father in outrage. "There's no such thing."

"But"—it suddenly occurs to him—"that's how it is with the Jews. No one can smell them, not anywhere."

*

Sirius has discovered a hole in the garden fence, between the elderberries and the hydrangeas, and he slips out through it whenever he's in the mood for some distraction.

He wanders through Berlin, in whatever direction the wind takes him, always taking care not to lose sight of the way back.

Where is this war that everyone is always talking about? Sirius imagines war to be loud and wild; like the shoot-out in the saloon at Luckyville, only bigger.

But instead the city is eerily quiet. The streets are empty, cars and buses are a rare sight. Gasoline has been rationed. People go to places on foot. They have gray, serious faces. They line up in front of the few shops which still exist, in the hope of getting some food in exchange for ration coupons. Meat and bread are rationed too.

At least he's been lucky in that sense, thinks Sirius. Hunger is not something he is suffering from. He is full to the bursting point with good German food, so much so that he feels ashamed.

By the side of the street, children trade bomb fragments with one another. They are from the last English air raid, which was a while ago now, when Sirius was still in Florida—in The Greatest Show on Earth.

The English bombers are threatening to come back soon. To be on the safe side, Berlin is making every structure possible into an air-raid shelter. Gas masks are being distributed to the population. Sirius has to brace himself now—for The Greatest War on Earth.

Why does fate drive him repeatedly to places where The "Greatest" is taking place at that very moment?

The "Small" can be nice too. Why not The Smallest Show in the World? Somewhere in Switzerland. Or The Smallest War in the World. Wishful thinking.

He just has to accept it: whatever he does, he'll always end up making it big.

Lost in thought, Sirius roams around. As directionless as his wanderings are, he always ends up being drawn back to his old home, as though guided by some invisible hand. He stands there before his tree.

"There you are again," says the tree, clearly delighted.

"Yes," answers Sirius, exhausted.

"How are you?" asks the tree.

"Well," sighs Sirius, "just look at my life."

"Always being hunted, always on the run," says the tree. "Ever since I've known you."

Sirius remains silent.

"I can't run," says the tree.

"You have roots," says Sirius, envying the tree for it.

Both of them ponder for a while the advantages and disadvantages of roots, giving particular consideration to the fact that trees don't have a choice in the matter, whereas dogs, by their very nature, are more mobile. Just imagine a tree on the run.

* * *

"Look who it is," cries the tree.

A man is approaching in the distance. He stops in his tracks and opens his eyes wide, unsure whether or not he is dreaming.

Sirius recognizes him at once, wagging his tail with joy and rushing over to him.

It's Benno Fritsche. Good old Uncle Benno.

"This can't be real!" whoops Fritsche, stretching both arms out wide. In his excitement, he drops his cane, which is intended to emphasize his dignified appearance. Benno Fritsche, actor, film star, Party member.

"I've been looking for you everywhere, little dog!" he cries, completely out of breath. "By order of Hollywood."

He gives a dramatic account of how inconsolable the family is, he gesticulates with both hands to show how many tears have flowed, he quotes from Rahel's countless letters about how all of Hollywood misses Hercules and how they're all counting on him, Uncle Benno, to search for the dog in Berlin.

Sirius is deeply moved. So they haven't forgotten him after all.

"The Second World War is, of course, the most foolish of moments to look for a missing dog," comments Fritsche. But he has succeeded.

He leans over to Sirius.

"Now be careful!" he whispers. "You're in danger, I can sense it. I'm in danger too, but more on that later. We can't be spotted together in public under any circumstances. Go back to where you came from. We'll meet every Wednesday after-noon at my house. But be careful! This is a secret mission!"

*

A new law comes into force, forbidding Jews from keeping pets. They are instructed to immediately put their dogs or cats to sleep. Germans are also forbidden from keeping Jewish pets.

Jewish pets? Erwin Wünsche wrinkles his brow. How do you recognize a Jewish pet? Does it hang its head sadly when it trots past a burned-down synagogue? Is it particularly lazy on Saturdays? Is its nose a different shape?

He is posing these questions in relation to Hansi, of course. The dog was a stray, after all, and he picked him up in good faith that he was a German dog.

Is it possible that what he actually found was a devious Jewish pet, pulling the wool over his eyes in order to escape being put down? If that were the case, Wünsche would be guilty of an offense. His career would be over.

Hansi is certainly no hunting dog; that makes him suspi-cious. On the other hand: he loves German sausage. Are Jews not kosher?

And so the Hauptsturmführer's thoughts go around in circles. He likes Hansi. Naturally, though, he would shoot him on the spot if the law required it. But it hasn't yet come to that.

He decides to take Hansi for a walk in front of the min-istry the next morning, very casually, right at the time when

Hermann Göring arrives for the day. No one can differentiate a German dog from a Jewish dog better than the Reichsmarschall.

The plan proves successful.

The imposing state carriage drives up, and out of it climbs the Reichsmarschall, dressed particularly smartly today. He is wearing a snow-white uniform with gold buttons and braid, and his chest is littered with orders and medals. Over his shoulders lies a fur sash that reaches down to the floor, presumably mink or chinchilla.

Seemingly by coincidence, Erwin Wünsche is standing on the grassy area in front of the drive. At the end of the lead is Hansi, in the process of lifting his leg over a cornflower.

"Wünsche," calls Göring in surprise, "what are you doing here? Are you not on duty today?"

The Hauptsturmführer salutes. "I'm always on duty, Herr Reichsmarschall! The German people are aware of their high moral obligation toward animals!"

"Bravo!" replies Göring, pleased that the preamble to his Reich Animal Protection Law is being put into practice.

"Is that your dog?" he asks.

"Yes, Herr Reichsmarschall," replies Wünsche. "Yes and no. He is everyone's dog. We follow the Führer! That applies to the German people and German dogs."

Göring nods in approval. "So what's the little chap's name?"

"Hansi, Herr Reichsmarschall," replies Wünsche.

"Hansi Herr Reichsmarschall?" smirks Göring. "That's a long name for such a little dog."

He winks to show that he's making a joke. Wünsche salutes, a little taken aback. It is intended to mean: joke understood.

Now the conversation becomes more serious. The Hauptsturmführer summons up his courage. "Herr Reichsmarschall, please allow me to ask you a question. One that only you, as the highest authority on German animals, can answer. Is Hansi a good dog?"

Göring feels flattered, and for this reason he wants to give the question due consideration.

He circles around Hansi, estimates his height and checks his tail. Then he pontificates: "The breed was reared by Prince Albrecht zu Solms-Braunfels, a noble Hessian family that goes back to the twelfth century. The lion is its heraldic animal.

"Hansi," he calls approvingly, "the blue blood of the Count Palatine runs in your veins. The stately castles of noble knights are your kennels."

Even his testicles don't escape an appraisal. Göring comes to his ceremonious conclusion: "Hansi, you are a good dog."

The dog can't help but feel a certain pride. Blue-blooded, who would have thought it? He has to admit that he's always had a weakness for accolades. In Hollywood he was given the "Golden Hercules." And now, for the role of Hansi, the seal of approval from the Reichsmarschall. A tragic role, therefore significantly more demanding.

This fills him with satisfaction.

Sirius is saved. For the time being, at least.

* * *

"Wünsche," says Göring, "it's actually very convenient that we should run into one another, as I was planning to speak to you anyway. And Hansi has strengthened my resolve. I have big plans for you.

"Your tomatoes," he continues, "are proof of your high regard for organic food. I haven't forgotten the five thousand nesting boxes, on the double. You are a man of action. And now I'm seeing that you're a dog lover too. All respect to you!"

The eulogist stretches his hand out into the German greeting.

"Hauptsturmführer Wünsche!" he exclaims. "What I have said qualifies you for the most responsible role there is in the Reich Chancellery. I'm promoting you to personal adjutant of the Führer!"

*

Wednesday afternoon. Sirius creeps out of the house and makes his way to Benno Fritsche's apartment, taking care that nobody sees him slip in through the garden gate.

Fritsche is not alone. He is surrounded by men smoking cigars and scowling worriedly. They call themselves the "Circle."

"This is Sirius," Fritsche introduces him.

"Welcome to the Circle," says Count von Studnitz. The other members of the Circle introduce themselves too, clearly not at all taken aback by the fact that a dog is joining their midst.

They know his story. An American in the group, called Ted Bloomfield, even knows his films.

"You saved Luckyville," he says. "Bravo!"

The others laugh.

"We want to save Germany," says Count von Studnitz. "Maybe you can help us with that."

Save Germany? Sirius gives a start. He has no idea how he could help with that.

"Does he have any idea what we're saying?" asks the man who introduced himself as Professor Wundt.

"He understands every word," says Fritsche. As proof, he lays two pieces of paper on the floor, one of which has "yes" written on it, and the other "no."

"Is today Tuesday?" asks Fritsche.

Sirius jumps on "no."

"Is today Wednesday?" calls Bloomfield.

Sirius jumps on "yes."

And so the questioning continues, until Professor Wundt triumphantly demands: "Does nothingness exist?"

Sirius jumps on "no."

"He's contradicting Nietzsche!" marvels Wundt.

"And he's right to!" retorts Count von Studnitz. "Nihilism was the beginning of the end!"

"Now, now," retorted Wundt, changing tack. "If anyone was right then it was Kierkegaard."

"We're going around in circles again," groans Bloomfield.

Sirius doesn't understand the circuitous debate. Is this why they are called the Circle?

Fritsche bangs his fist down on the table.

"Listen, all of you!" he cries. "You're making the dog nervous. He must think we're all crazy."

"Sirius," says Count von Studnitz in a calm tone, "we are the Circle. We are an underground organization. We are in the resistance. Do you understand what I mean?"

Sirius jumps on the paper with "no."

"Germany is in the hands of monsters," reinforces Wundt. "That's what we're fighting against."

"Monsters!" repeats Bloomfield. "Exactly!"

Sirius jumps on "yes."

The poor dog is utterly confused. All he wanted was to pay a visit to Uncle Benno, his erstwhile knight in shining armor, the familiar face on the advertising pillars.

"I was the poster boy!" laments Fritsche. "I gave my face to this evil spectacle. And what do I see when I look in the mirror? A mask. A lie."

"Keep your voice down!" admonishes Count von Studnitz. He has to prevent the dissenter from being too obvious about his resistance. Being underground is not Fritsche's strong suit.

Sirius is tired. He wants to go home.

"We know that you live in the house of a Hauptsturm-führer," whispers Bloomfield. "You'll be sure to hear something here and there that could be of interest to us."

"We help you, and you help us," says Count von Studnitz.

*

The letter with the swastika seal arrives in Hollywood like a missive from hell. And that's exactly what it is.

The Crown family is so happy that Sirius is alive. And yet, the letter closes with the words "There is nothing you can do for your beloved dog now except pray. He is in the service of our Fatherland. With love, Benno."

Fatherland? Not even Jack Warner, Hercules's creator, could have imagined that the little dog was currently poised to save Germany. The script said ancient Rome, but Berlin is his fate.

The summer is drawing to a close. Else and Andreas welcome their child into the world, a boy, Johnny. The proud grandparents are filled with joy.

Georg has completed his medical studies. He is now an intern in a practice in Santa Monica.

But there is no light without shadow. Carl Crown is summoned to see Jack Warner. Even as he steps into the office, he already has what people call an "uneasy feeling." And it proves to be well-founded.

"Any news on the dog?" asks Warner gruffly.

Crown launches into a story which is supposed to end with the bit about the service to the Fatherland.

"Where's the dog?" bellows Warner.

Crown asks for his understanding regarding the Second World War; Hitler wanted it, so Berlin has no choice but to be part of it all.

"Enough about Hitler," interrupts Warner angrily. "That man has already unleashed enough misery, and the dog plays no part in it. But here in the studio, the dog does play a part. The lead part—Hercules!"

He thinks for a moment, his mind racing.

"The world," he says after a while, "wants Hercules. It's irrelevant who plays the dog. Find a dog that looks like your dog! A doppelgänger."

Crown is outraged. "A doppelgänger? Impossible. There isn't one, Sirius is unique."

"Unique?" roars Warner. "Nonsense. Every dog is replaceable."

"Not Sirius," says Crown, firmly and abruptly.

Jack Warner stares at him with the ice-cold eyes of a shark cheated out of its prey. Then he makes the kind of hand gesture with which someone might swat away a fly.

"Leave the Chevrolet in the courtyard. And vacate that strange glass house of yours. Immediately."

In the blink of an eye, Carl Crown has become jobless and homeless.

*

Erwin Wünsche begins his position in the Reich Chancellery. The Führer's quarters are located on the first floor. Willy Kannenberg, the so-called house intendant, is responsible for the Führer's housekeeping. He briefs Wünsche on his new role.

"The first job of the morning is to iron the world map," he says. "The Führer hates it when the world map is creased."

Wünsche makes a note.

"Breakfast," continues Kannenberg. "The Führer goes to

bed late and rises late. Krause, the valet, will give you the
signal. Crispbread, butter, honey, cocoa. Always the same
thing. But Lange, the cook, knows all of that."

Wünsche makes a note.

"On the stroke of twelve o' clock, Julius Schaub will read
out the schedule for the day. Schaub is the Führer's chief
adjutant and your immediate superior. The schedule, of
course, is dependent on the Führer's appointments. Essentially
speaking, you are responsible for everything that moves.
That's easy enough to remember."

"But," Wünsche hesitates, "when you think about it
everything moves, in a way."

"Does it?" asks Kannenberg. He points at the chandelier.
"Is that moving right now, in your eyes?"

"No," admits Wünsche.

Kannenberg nods solemnly. "Correct. So you are not
responsible for it. Five things move, generally speaking.
Tires, pictures, Blondi, breakfast and the front."

Wünsche makes a note.

"Tires," explains Kannenberg, "means the fleet of vehicles. Erich Kempka is the Führer's chauffeur. Pictures. I
mean moving pictures. The Führer likes to watch films in
the evening. Blondi. The Führer's dog. She needs a lot of
movement."

"Understood," says Wünsche. "I have a dog myself."

"No, no," corrects Kannenberg, "the walking is taken
care of by Paul Feni, Blondi's keeper. You are the contact
person. You coordinate. Vet appointments. Transport. To
the Berghof, to the Wolf's Lair. That kind of thing."

Wünsche makes a note.

"So what's left?" asks Kannenberg, checking the newcomer's quick-wittedness.

"Breakfast and the front!" calls Wünsche.

"Correct," comes the answer. "Breakfast is taken to the Führer. It is the only meal which he likes to eat alone. For lunch and dinner he dines in company. Now, the front . . ."

Wünsche interrupts, startled. "I hope I'm not responsible for the soldiers on the front. I mean, they're moving, after all."

"Of course not," Kannenberg reassures him. "The Führer himself takes care of that. Your job, as I already mentioned, is to iron the map of the world."

"But I don't see where the movement is," says Wünsche assiduously. "In what way does the map of the world move?"

"It crinkles," replies Kannenberg.

*

Air-raid siren. The English bombers are coming back. In the middle of the night, the sirens suddenly begin to wail.

The ear-piercing sound tears the Wünsches from a deep sleep. They lie in bed fully dressed at night, and have done so ever since the high alert was given on the radio. The suitcase stands packed and ready by the front door. So they are out on the street in a matter of moments and on their way to the nearest air-raid shelter.

The planes are already circling in the sky, dropping flares designed to illuminate the targets for the bombers. Immediately in their wake follow the deadly war planes with explosives and firebombs.

*   *   *

The bunker at Bahnhof Zoo can accommodate eighteen thousand people, and yet it is still a matter of luck that the Wünsches are able to find shelter at the last minute. The crush is intense and any space has long since been filled.

"No pets!" bellows the air-raid warden at the entrance. He means Sirius.

Erwin Wünsche protests—but in vain. The warden remains firm.

"No pets! No Jews! We don't even have enough space for people!"

Sirius has to stay outside.

The fear in the bunker chokes throats shut. The heat is stifling. The stench of the burning city forces its way into the cellar through the air vents. Gertrud trembles with fear, clinging on to her husband. He is as pale as a corpse, staring at the concrete ceiling as it tremors more dangerously with every explosion. The bombs are falling right above them. Ulrich and Rudi cry, pressing their hands against their ears.

Sirius trots along the Kurfürstendamm. He could creep into a doorway, he could seek shelter under a bridge, he could flee into a cellar.

But no. He walks right in the middle of the street. The pyrotechnics of the phosphorus bombs illuminate the night sky. The glowing splinters set trees on fire. The theater on Kurfürstendamm goes up in flames, the German Opera House on Bismarkstrasse, the university. The Deutschlandhalle arena is burning.

Sirius walks through the sea of flames. Proud and brave. He isn't afraid of the Allies' hailstorm of bombs.

And why would he be? After all, he is their ally.

*

In Stalingrad, the fate of the German Wehrmacht turns within a matter of days. The Sixth Army has almost completely destroyed the city, and Hitler is already celebrating the victory of Operation Hubertus with a frenetic speech in the Löwenbräukeller beer hall in Munich.

But at the last moment, the Red Army makes a success of Operation Uranus, the counteroffensive. They encircle the enemy, and suddenly the German army is trapped. The Russian winter rages. The soldiers freeze and starve.

Hermann Göring, the supreme commander of the Luftwaffe, has announced Operation Winter Storm, the aerial rescue mission. But he is unable to make good on his promise. The Stalingrad cauldron becomes a deadly trap. A German soldier dies every seven seconds.

While this is happening, Erwin Wünsche irons around the Volga on the map of the world with particular precision. Under no circumstances can the front line be allowed to crumple.

Krause, the valet, tiptoes over and gives the signal for breakfast. Lange, the cook, has laid out crispbreads, butter, honey and cocoa on the tray. The door opens, and out steps the Führer.

Erwin Wünsche finds himself standing right before Hitler for the first time. He stands to attention.

The Führer is a man whose side parting doesn't sit quite right first thing in the morning, his hair is disheveled, and even his famous mustache doesn't have its distinctive shape until after his shave. He is wearing a dressing gown, and his feet are encased in slippers with the swastika emblem. For breakfast, he puts on his peaked cap with its wreath of oak leaves. He yawns.

"Is this the young man we have Göring to thank for?" he asks.

Wünsche salutes. *"Ja, mein Führer!"*

The Führer looks exhausted. The previous evening, he held one of his frequent monologues on the international situation deep into the night. His guests, fed with overcooked vegetables and unable to get a word in edgewise, are witnesses of the so-called Table Talk. As always at these events, the Führer's thoughts are captured for posterity by a stenographer.

The evenings usually come to an end in the at-home cinema, where the Führer likes to unwind by watching Hollywood movies. Yesterday it was Walt Disney's *Snow White*, his favorite.

"What do we have today?" he asks, pointing his crispbread at the man who is responsible for moving pictures. Wünsche, already familiar with the Führer's tastes, suggests Laurel and Hardy.

"Very good," says the Führer approvingly.

The red light on the telephone illuminates, which means there is a call for the Führer. A highly unusual occurrence at this time of the morning. Everyone knows that the Führer's official working day begins only once he has taken up residence, fresh and alert, at his desk in the Reich Chancellery. Right now, he is still sitting at breakfast in his robe.

"Colonel General Paulus," whispers Rochus Misch, the bodyguard, and hands over the receiver.

Bad news on the Stalingrad cauldron. The Führer rolls his eyes. "*Ja ja*," he says, now and again. Then he bellows: "Retreat? That's not an option. Persevere, and that's an order!" Then he hangs up.

"Herr Wollenhaupt is here," announces the valet. The Führer's barber has arrived to trim his mustache.

*

Every Wednesday, Sirius goes to Benno Fritsche's house. The Circle has realized that the dog's appearance in their lives was a great stroke of luck. His master is the Führer's personal adjutant and brings home the latest news from the Reich Chancellery each evening—and the dog listens in.

Now the bearer of this sensitive information just needs to learn how to divulge his knowledge. They remember Kurwenal, the famous dachshund who was able to read and write.

Why not? Professor Wundt, the expert within the Circle, offers himself as a teacher. As chance would have it, he even once met the founder of New Animal Psychology, Mathilde Freiin von Freytag-Loringhoven. She was the one who taught Kurwenal how to speak via barked code.

But that won't work in this case. "Too loud," Count von Studnitz points out. The neighbors might get suspicious.

Ted Bloomfield, the American, suggests the construction of an enormous typewriter, with each key large enough for the dog to press with his paw. "Like a piano," he says.

"Why not an actual piano?" ponders Wundt. "With every key representing a letter."

"Just imagine the clatter it would make," shudders Count von Studnitz. "An absolute cacophony."

"So what?" says Benno Fritsche. "Surely practicing the piano is still allowed around here."

"Not if it sounds like Arnold Schönberg," says Bloomfield in amusement. "He had to go into exile after his piano concerto."

The Circle decides to give it a go with the instrument. Professor Wundt will train Sirius, on the piano, to be a spy.

By the time of their next meeting, there is already a black piano in the house. The keys are marked with letters, the hammers fitted with a mute. Sirius is to play *con sordino*.

The concert sounds rather strange, admittedly. The professor explains the basic rules of phonetics by uttering drawn-out vocals, and Sirius accompanies him on the piano.

The others encircle the two musicians, as is befitting of a group called the Circle. They listen eagerly to see how Sirius will take to his new task.

Will it work? Who knows. In any case, it will be a little while before the dog is even able to spell the word "Hitler" using music.

* * *

When Benno Fritsche bumps into Frau Zinke a few days later, she asks curiously: "Have you taken up the piano recently?"

Benno Fritsche bows humbly. "One does what one can. Or can't, as the case may be."

"I thought you were playing jazz," says Frau Zinke. "That would be forbidden."

"Jazz?" says Fritsche with theatrical outrage. "No, I only play Beethoven."

Frau Zinke has learned something new again. "Ah, is that how it sounds? I imagined it to be different."

Fritsche takes off his hat in farewell, then raises his index finger and says: "Every line etched by sorrow wanes, as long as music's enchantment reigns. Schiller."

*

"Christmas trees! Christmas trees!" cries the seller in front of the drugstore in Hollywood. "Make you happy. Better than any drug."

Rahel pauses and looks at the man. He gives her a friendly nod. She shakes her head, her eyes filling with tears. Without a word, she continues on her way.

Happiness is a thing of yesterday. Carl and Rahel have lost everything. They stand there empty-handed, just like when they first arrived in Hollywood. Are they at the end? Or the beginning? Who knows?

Else and Andreas have taken the two of them into their home. Their apartment is really only just big enough for their young happiness. But now the misfortune of the old has to fit in too. The poor parents sleep in the child's room that was intended for Johnny. His bed is in the living room. There is no space left for a Christmas tree. Only for a sprig of fir in a vase at the very most.

Christmas Eve in the smallest of spaces, in the greatest adversity.

Georg and Electra come too. They have become inseparable. Andreas fetches another two chairs from the kitchen.

"Lovely apartment," says Electra politely.

"But small," apologizes Else.

"Space is relative," comforts Electra. An insight that she hasn't just picked up from the seminars of Bertrand Russell. Her father is Conrad Nicholson Hilton, the hotel mogul. There is always plenty of room at the Hiltons'.

Carl defiantly launches into a rendition of "O Christmas Tree." He puts the emphasis on the word "tree," not without an undertone of bitterness. Johnny hears his grandfather singing for the first time; it scares him, and he cries.

The family is together. If not beneath a Christmas tree, then at least next to the sprig of fir, upon which a candle is valiantly trying to cast a festive ambience. The only thing missing is Sirius.

They remember him with a minute of silence. May God protect him. May his light always shine, wherever he is. The candle flickers, as though their whispered prayer has been heard.

As it happens, Sirius really is thinking of his far-away family at this very moment. Merry Christmas, he wishes them. Is the sheriff with them again, he wonders?

No, not the sheriff as well in that tiny apartment, please.

"Hansi!" calls the stern voice of the Hauptsturmführer, tearing the dog from his thoughts.

The Wünsches have a Christmas tree, of course. It's in the garden, and flourishes not only in the summertime, but in the winter too, when it snows. The family pull on their boots and stomp outside. The white finery is the most beautiful decoration the branches can have.

"Merry Christmas!" commands the patriarch.

Then they have roast duck. Another one of the privileges that come with being the Führer's adjutant.

The special Christmas program is on the Volksempfänger radio. It begins with the festive bell ringing of the German cathedrals, then connects the soldiers on the front and the people back at home in a reverent celebration of Christmas Eve.

"Attention everyone!" crackles the moderator's static voice. "I will now hand over to our comrades, who will speak to you from the most far-flung of locations. I am now calling the Arctic harbor of Liinahamari."

The soldiers in the Arctic Circle come onto the air, their teeth chattering with cold, and greet their families back home.

"Attention," announces the static voice of the moderator once more, "I am now calling Stalingrad!"

The soldiers in the cauldron wish everyone a Merry Christmas.

The program continues with greetings from Tunis, Catania, Crete, Marseille, Zakopane and the Bay of Biscay.

"From all over the world!" marvels Ulrich.

"You see," replies his mother proudly. "That's why it's called a world war."

Next up are the soldiers in the Crimean Peninsula. As if on command, the men strike up the Christmas song "Silent Night."

The moderator is moved. "This spontaneous gesture from our comrades far away on the Black Sea has now united all the transmission stations around the world."

"Holy infant so tender and mild" resounds out ever more wholeheartedly, with ever more voices joining in.

"Now they're singing in the Arctic Circle," rejoices the moderator. "Now they're singing in the combat zone in Rzhev. Now we'll switch to Stalingrad. And now France. Now Africa is singing too."

"And now all of you at home," he cries, "sing along!"

*

The Führer has returned from spending the holidays in Upper Salzburg, so the service of Adjutant Wünsche begins once more.

Blondi stays behind in the Berghof for now. Why would the dog want to be in the gloomy Reich Chancellery, when instead he could be out romping in the open air with Negus and Stasi, Eva Braun's terriers?

Perfectly understandable, but now the Führer is sitting there without a dog, and that puts him in a surly mood. He loves dogs. Nothing cheers him up like having a dog around to teach bizarre tricks to.

Even after so much time has passed, he still enthuses now and then about Fuchsl, the little stray terrier he encountered in Alsace back when he was just a simple soldier, on leave from the front. Fuchsl was smart and quick to learn. Before long, he was able to clamber up a ladder on all fours. One witness of this performance had offered two hundred Deutschmarks for the dog. "I wouldn't give him up even for two hundred thousand Deutschmarks," came Hitler's answer. Soon after that, Fuchsl suddenly vanished without a trace. The column had to go back to the front, the master without his dog. A tragedy.

Blondi cannot climb ladders. And why would she? She's a German shepherd, not a circus clown. How times change; Hitler is no longer a simple soldier, but the Führer. He needs a dog that represents something. A dog that proudly represents his race.

Officially, the Führer poses happily with Blondi. But in secret, he longs for Fuchsl.

"Ah, Fuchsl," sighs the Führer woefully. "Bring me the map of the world, Wünsche."

Wünsche brings the map of the world. The Führer pushes his index finger across Alsace, murmuring place-names from long-forgotten times: Sundgau, Mulhausen, Schiltigheim.

"Here!" he calls. "Horndorf! That's where I lost him."

Wünsche stands there in sympathetic silence. He contemplates in all seriousness whether the erstwhile stray Hansi could possibly be Fuchsl, having trotted from Horndorf to Berlin in the search for his master. No, that would make Hansi—wait a moment—thirty years old. Impossible. Or was it?

"Thirty years," ventures Wünsche. "Maybe he's still alive."

"Nonsense," grumbles the Führer. "You know nothing about dogs."

Wünsche, timidly: "I have a dog."

"Oh really?" says the Führer. "What kind?"

Wünsche describes Hansi. The shaggy fur, spotted white and brown, the perky ears, the long snout, the cheerful tail.

"Like Fuchsl!" cries the Führer, moved.

Wünsche permits himself to respectfully make the observation that the Reichsmarschall himself declared Hansi to be a good dog, commenting on the pedigree that stretches back to the twelfth century.

"That's very impressive," says the Führer. "Bring Hansi by to see me when you get the chance."

Has Wünsche heard correctly? Adolf Hitler, the Führer of the German people, the greatest field commander of all time, has personally addressed him, Erwin Wünsche? From one dog lover to another, so to speak? His chest swells with pride.

Hansi should get a nice reward for making this possible. The cook agrees and hands over a big piece of sausage. Führer sausage.

That evening, it is handed over ceremoniously.

* * *

"My dear Hansi," begins Wünsche in a solemn tone. "Your name came up today during a conversation with the Führer."

Gertrud claps her hands over her mouth in disbelief.

"The Führer and I," he continues, "we talked about you. And I'll emphasize that point: we talked. You brought us, the Führer and I, closer together on a human level. I emphasize again: on a human level."

As a sign of his appreciation, he unwraps the sausage and lays it by the dog's feet.

Ulrich and Rudi stare entranced at their father, who has suddenly taken on historical dimensions. The Führer and I. The dog too, they see with new eyes. He is the hero of the day.

"And wait for it!" says the father. "The Führer wants to make your personal acquaintance, Hansi!"

Gertrud expresses her amazement by dropping her jaw and sitting there open-mouthed. She is speechless.

The dog which no one at home knows what to do with is suddenly a welcome guest in the Führer's headquarters.

*

Dr. Joseph Goebbels, the Minister for Propaganda, has the floor. He is addressing the German people in the Berlin Sportpalast.

"The German people," he says, "have to defend their most holy assets: their families, their women and children, their beautiful and pristine landscape, their towns and villages, the two-thousand-year legacy of their culture, and everything that makes life worth living."

Then he becomes enraged. At the lords and archbishops in London, at international Bolshevism, at the sham civilization of Judaism, at the stampede of the steppe toward our honorable continent. At everything.

"I ask you," roars Goebbels, "do you want total war? If necessary, do you want a war more total and radical than anything that we can even imagine today?"

The answer is a tumultuous "*Ja!*" from thousands of throats. A hurricane of applause.

The speech is being broadcast on the radio, which, in the words of its orator, means that "millions of people are connected to us here in this room over the airwaves."

Including the Circle.

"Now they have truly lost their minds," says Count von Studnitz, shaking his head.

"We have just been listening to the devil," declares Benno Fritsche. "Mephisto."

"The devil's mouthpiece," calls Bloomfield. "Hitler is the true devil!"

Sirius flinches. He still has the scent of that sausage in his nose. Was it the sausage of the devil? Does the devil himself want to meet him? A shiver runs down his spine.

Professor Wundt is no longer able to stay seated; he paces nervously back and forth, stirred up by the vile speech.

"We really have to take action," he says. "Hitler must go!"

But how? Bloomfield reports on the plans of the Heidinger Circle, friends of theirs, who are plotting to shoot Hitler. Another possibility being considered is a bomb to fire Hitler into the air.

"All we're missing is one link in the chain, but unfortunately it's the decisive one," says Bloomfield. "An informant close to Hitler. Our man in the Führer's headquarters."

Is it possible that it could be a dog? How Sirius longs to be able to cry out: "Me! I'm going to meet the Führer in person soon! He has already sent me a sausage! Maybe I can help you."

But he can't talk. Not yet.

Excited, he jumps up onto the piano and bashes the keys.

"He's trying to tell us something!" cries Benno in amazement.

The Circle listens, captivated. Professor Wundt translates letter after letter.

"Hitler. Sausage."

"His first words," whispers Count von Studnitz, deeply moved.

"What do you think they mean?" asks Bloomfield.

The men retreat conspiratorially back to their armchairs, light up cigars and ponder. Is the dog's message to be understood as a commentary on the Führer's personality, something along the lines of him being a "silly sausage"?

"He's right, you know," says the Count. "But a highly dangerous one."

It is, of course, also plausible that the words are meant symbolically, like a poem in which "sausage" quite simply stands for something that is worth *striving for*, like *salvation*. Save us from Hitler!

"From the dog's perspective, that would make sense," comments the professor. "Think about it—he spoke the words just after we mentioned the Hitler assassination plot."

"Or perhaps the dog just means he hasn't found anything yet. Not a sausage," says Bloomfield.

Fritsche frowns. "Then do you think this is going to help us? We need to get some inside information as soon as we can."

"I'm just saying," Bloomfield reassures him. "We have to consider all the possible interpretations."

Sirius feels misunderstood. One thing is certain; he needs to learn to express himself more clearly as quickly as he can.

*

In Hollywood, fate is turning again, and for the better. The happy twist was prompted by Electra. Quite simply, she electrifies.

"Do something for the Crowns, Daddy, won't you?" she asked her father.

Conrad Nicholson Hilton actually has his mind on other matters. He has just bought the Waldorf-Astoria and the Plaza in New York, the two crown jewels, and with them he wants to become the Hotel King of America. He is also newly wed to Zsa Zsa Gabor, which is no easy task in itself. So he has little time to devote to two people who are unable to get over the loss of their dog.

"For my sake," begs Electra, "please!"

Her joyous smile has bewitched philosophers, and now it

turns out that even kings are defenseless to her charms, not to mention fathers.

"Stop giggling," says Hilton. "You know very well I can't say no when you giggle."

And it's a good thing he can't. Carl Crown, as a result, is now working as a porter in the newly opened Hilton hotel, The Townhouse, in Beverly Hills. For Rahel, the position of hostess was created. She welcomes the guests and tends to their needs. The Crowns live in the hotel now too.

Crown wears a Bordeaux-red uniform with gold bobbles, along with a matching cap. Rahel wears a uniform in the same color, and beneath it a white blouse with the hotel emblem.

Else is unprepared for the sight when she visits her parents for the first time in their new home. Tears of emotion fill her eyes. The way her father bravely stands tall beneath his cap, the way her mother stands ready to greet guests with the coat of arms on her chest—it's heart-wrenching.

"I know," says Crown, with a smile, "I look like an eggplant."

"You both look wonderful!" cries Else. "Like something from a movie. *Made in Hollywood.*"

"It really is like the movies," says Rahel. "We were put out on the street, and suddenly we're living in a palace with a hundred rooms."

Crown nods valiantly.

The revolving door sets into motion, and in comes a man who scours the room for familiar faces with a practiced gaze, before heading toward Crown with his eyes and arms wide.

"Who is this I see before me?" he cries.

It's John Clark. On his way to the hotel bar, of course, which is alleged to be the best bar in town. He looks the Bordeaux-red Crown up and down, wrinkling his brow.

"Is this the new guardian angel uniform?" he inquires.

"On the contrary," replies Crown. "I have my guardian angel to thank for the uniform."

Clark looks puzzled. "You'll have to explain that one to me. Let's go and have a drink!"

After the end of his shift, Crown follows him into the bar. He is looking forward to pouring out his heart to his friend from the good old days.

There's a lot to tell. The circus in Florida. Manzini and the time machine. The Turk. Berlin. Hercules. Hitler. Hilton.

John Clark tries to follow.

"Oh man," he says, "I don't get it. Maybe I'm already too drunk."

"Hercules is in Berlin!" exclaims Crown.

"That's crazy!" replies Clark. "I'm shooting a movie with him right now, in ancient Egypt. *Hercules and Cleopatra*."

"What?" cries Crown. "Jack Warner, that sly dog! It's his doppelgänger!"

"Who is whose doppelgänger?" asks John Clark.

Sometimes life is just too complicated.

*

The Führer has recovered from the annihilation of the Sixth Army at Stalingrad. He is in a better mood again, especially now that the uprising in the Warsaw ghetto has been quashed.

So why not take the dog along one of these days, like the Führer suggested?

Wünsche puts the lead on Hansi, while Gertrud combs him down beautifully one more time.

Their stroll to the Führer's headquarters is bathed in sunshine. One can feel that springtime is on its way. The first trees are beginning to blossom. Wünsche lets the dog take his time around the tree trunks; he needs him to have an empty bladder when he meets the Führer. Heaven forbid he should cause that kind of mischief.

The Führer is already sitting at his desk when they arrive. His hands rest on the ebony intarsia of a brandished sword.

"Look who it is," he calls cheerfully, "the doggy."

"*Mein Führer*, may I present Hansi," Wünsche says, saluting.

The Führer gets up and pats the dog on the head. "Good doggy," he says repeatedly. "Now then, let's see what you can do, Hansi."

He takes off the lead, positions himself directly in front of Hansi, stretches his index finger up high and commands, "Down!"

Hansi lies down obediently on the floor.

"Good doggy," he says. Then he points his finger at his chair and calls, "Up!"

Hansi jumps up onto the chair and sits enthroned at the

desk where the Führer was sitting only moments before. He lays his paw theatrically on the sword intarsia.

The Führer doubles over with laughter.

The dog feels uneasy. This is the man he has spent his whole life fleeing from. The man who made his entire world go up in flames. And now he is sitting opposite him, playing with fire. A dangerous game.

The door connecting the office to the waiting room opens, and the secretary announces: "Admiral Canaris, *mein Führer*!"

Canaris, the Chief of military Intelligence, steps into the room and is stunned to see a dog sitting at the desk—and in exactly the same pose as the Führer, to top it all off.

"Don't worry, there hasn't been a coup!" snorts the Führer.

"That's good to know," responds Canaris, his expression impenetrable. "I have important news."

The Führer takes his seat again. The dog settles down by his feet.

"We've gathered intelligence," reports Canaris, "that the Allied invasion isn't planned for Sicily, as we thought."

"Not Sicily?" The Führer gapes in amazement. "Then where?"

"Sardinia," says Canaris. "Our troops need to be withdrawn from Sicily at once and stationed in Sardinia."

"What kind of intelligence?" the Führer demands to know.

"A briefcase," says Canaris. "It was attached to a chain, and the chain was attached to a man. His body was washed up onto land in southern Spain. The man was a major in the British Royal Marines. The files testify conclusively that it's Sardinia."

"Heavens!" cries the Führer. "That's unbelievable."

"I know," says Canaris. "Unbelievable, but true."

The Führer slams his hand down on the table, incensed. "Right, then," he roars. "So Eisenhower and Montgomery want to take us for fools! They want us to think: North Africa, they're there already, and it's only a hop, skip and a jump across to Sicily. It seems so obvious! And we Germans will be sure to fall for it, right? And meanwhile they land in Sardinia and laugh themselves silly. Is that it?"

"That's it, yes," says Canaris.

"Fine then," shrills the Führer in a tremulous tone, taking perverse delight in his words. "Then they're in for the shock of their lives! We'll be waiting for their lordships in Sardinia!"

Admiral Canaris salutes. "What is your order, *mein Führer*?"

"Order General Field Marshal Kesselring to move the troops from Sicily to Sardinia. And inform Mussolini."

*

Sirius, therefore, has exciting news to report that following Wednesday, and luckily he really can report by now. He has made progress on the piano.

The Circle can see that the dog is almost bursting with his news: instead of making himself comfortable as usual, he rushes immediately over to the instrument.

* * *

"Was in Führer headquarters," he taps out. "Met Hitler."

"Met Hitler?" cries the professor, thunderstruck. "I can barely believe it."

"Met Hitler," confirms Sirius. "In person."

He describes the encounter with the staccato of his paws. The Circle listens reverently, as though a medium in a trance had established a connection with the other side.

Suddenly, the Führer is speaking through Sirius. Top secret words which influence the world from behind the dense walls of the Reich Chancellery have found their wondrous way into the ears of a dog, and then onto the keys of a piano. And the enemy is listening in.

Canaris. Sicily. Sardinia.

Ted Bloomfield listens intently. He asks Sirius for absolute precision. "Even the smallest detail is important," he says. "This is a sensation!"

Sirius reports of the dead British major who was fished out of the sea in Huelva, of the briefcase on the chain, of the files with the intelligence: the planned invasion of Sardinia.

"And?" asks Bloomfield nervously. "Reaction?"

Order. Troops. Sardinia.

"Really?" cries Bloomfield. "Withdrawal from Sicily?"

Sirius confirms. Order. Troops. Sardinia.

Bloomfield jumps up, throws his hands in the air and rejoices: "Victory! Victory! It worked. It worked! Operation Mincemeat was a success!"

"What worked?" asks Count von Studnitz, dumbfounded. Fritsche and Wundt are also staring at each other in confusion.

Bloomfield needs to regain his composure again before he speaks. It is not the first time that he knows more than the others in the Circle. Exactly why this is, he is unable to divulge, as he always says. But according to his insinuations, he has a direct link to the British secret service.

"Operation Mincemeat," he explains, "the dead major is a trick. A red herring. MI5 thought it up. All the documents were faked. They were intended to lead Hitler down the wrong path."

"So it is Sicily then, after all," Benno Fritsche says, catching on. "And now Hitler is withdrawing his troops."

"I can't say any more than that," adds Bloomfield mysteriously. "Just one thing. The big question was: Will the message reach Hitler? And if it does, will he fall for it? Now, thanks to Sirius, this question has been answered in the affirmative. Churchill will be very pleased."

Sirius feels proud. His message will please Churchill. He has not only met the Führer in person, but personally double-crossed him. There's not much more one could ask of a little Jewish dog, he thinks to himself.

The following day, the British prime minister receives a telegram with the words: "Mincemeat swallowed whole."

"How do we know for sure?" asks Churchill.

"From a reliable source," comes the answer. "We have a spy directly beneath Hitler's desk."

"Excuse me?" responds Churchill. "Are you serious?"
"Very much so," comes the answer. "A living micro-phone. A dog."
"A four-legged resistance fighter," says Churchill with a smile. "A dog in the lion's den. What a brave chap."

*

Sirius—no, Hansi—is now a regular visitor to the Reich Chancellery. The Führer "dotes" on the doggy, as he himself puts it. Ideally, he would have Hansi with him all the time. Even Bormann, his deputy, and Ribbentrop, his foreign minister, have by now grown accustomed to the fact that the dog is always present at their strategy meetings.

In the middle of a May meeting, to which the news is delivered that the Africa Corps in Tunisia has had to surrender, the Führer tells Hansi to sit up and beg.

"Look, Rommel!" says the Führer enthusiastically to Field Marshal Rommel.

"I don't know whether that will be of much use to our soldiers in Africa," grumbles Rommel. "I've said all along that we should have retreated from the desert."

"Well, it helps me," responds the Führer. "You could learn a lot from this dog's optimism!"

Ribbentrop and Rommel stare at each other in disbelief.

The Führer even goes so far as to ask the dog's advice on military matters. In the situation report in June, at which Field Marshal von Manstein is present, Operation Citadel is up for discussion. The subject is the attack on the Russian city of Kursk.

The last chance for a major offensive against the Red Army.

The military staff advise against it. The Führer turns to Hansi. "What do you think?" he asks.

The dog waves his tail. The Führer listens to him, and the greatest tank battle in history is unleashed. The German Wehrmacht is about to go through hell.

In July, the Allies land in Sicily. Not Sardinia. The German troops have been outwitted. "Fortress Europe" is beginning to waver. Mussolini is deposed.

The Führer is depressed. Even his closest confidantes are now expressing doubt on the "Final Victory." Only Hansi can comfort him.

"Good doggy," says the Führer. "You understand me. You are the only one who understands me."

If he only knew. The doggy does understand him, and word for word. Every Wednesday, he has his piano lesson, and the Circle finds out the latest developments. Thanks to him, even Churchill ends up understanding the Führer.

In August, Sirius brings warning of the so-called Wonder Weapon, the V-2 rocket which is being developed at the Peenemünde military research center. The Royal Air Force immediately bombs the site.

In September, Sirius reports the planned occupation of Rome. Code name of the operation: Case Axis. But the

Allies don't succeed in preventing the abduction of Mussolini. In October, Sirius has his greatest coup yet: he delivers news of Operation Steinbock. This is the code name for the planned bombing of London, scheduled for January.

The font of information in the Führer headquarters is positively bubbling. Sirius has become the Allies' most important spy.

In November, when Churchill meets the president of the United States in Cairo, Roosevelt asks curiously: "Who is this super spy, anyway?"

Churchill replies: "You'll laugh. A dog. In Berlin."

Roosevelt furrows his brow. "Hang on a moment. A dog in Berlin? Then I think I know who that is. There's no other dog it could be. Hercules!"

Sirius is now making world history.

And very speedily too. Every Wednesday, his paws glide nimbly over the piano keys. No longer staccato, but *molto furioso*.

When Frau Zinke runs into Benno Fritsche again, she seems very impressed.

"You played particularly beautifully today!" she says approvingly. "Beethoven again?"

"Who else?" answers Fritsche with his most charming wink.

*

Yet it hasn't escaped the German counterintelligence office that there must be a leak in the Führer's headquarters. And quite a considerable leak, as state secrets are literally gushing out of it.

Where could it be? And more to the point: *Who* could it be?

Admiral Canaris makes the investigation a top priority. As with everything else that is planned at the highest level with the greatest degree of secrecy, the action needs a code name. What could it be? The Führer loves names from the animal world. Operation Steinbock, Operation Sea Lion, Operation Arctic Fox. Why not Operation Hansi? It has a good ring to it.

There isn't even a hint of suspicion regarding the dog, of course. How could a dog pass on state secrets?

His master, however, is much more worthy of suspicion. Didn't the espionage start at exactly the time Erwin Wünsche began his service there? To do things by the book: Traudl Junge, the Führer's secretary, also had her first working day around this time. And Julius Manti, the new man in the Führer's team of guards.

Canaris thinks hard. Beforehand they didn't have the leak, and afterward they did. So one of the three is the traitor. Period. It's a good thing he put himself in charge of the investigation, otherwise there wouldn't have been results this quickly.

"*Mein Führer,*" he declares, "here is my report on Operation Hansi."

He presents the names of the three suspects. Traudl Junge is excluded; she wasn't present during the situation reports. Nor is Manti a viable suspect. He was only there occasionally, so he can't possibly have betrayed everything. That leaves Erwin Wünsche.

"True," says the Führer with distrust lurking in his voice. "He's always loitering around here, that man. Under the pretense of being the doggy's master."

"To be fair," Canaris comments, "it is his job to be present. He's your personal adjutant, *mein Führer*."

"I suppose that's true," ponders the Führer out loud, "but for some reason I never warmed to him. The two-faced trickster's up to something, you can feel it. He and the dog don't quite fit together. There's something not quite right."

"So there you are, *mein Führer*," attests Canaris. "Your instinct has never failed you."

"Have the man executed!" orders the Führer. "Immediately!"

"Executed?" says Canaris in shock. "Don't we need some clear evidence first?"

"My instinct is evidence enough," retorts the Führer. "But fine, if that's what you think. Summon him here."

Wünsche is brought in. Flanked by two officers of the SS Death's Head Unit.

"*Mein Führer!*" salutes Wünsche.

"'*Mein Führer!*'" sneers the Führer. "Give it a rest with the two-faced whining."

Wünsche trembles.

"You have betrayed the German Reich to the enemy!" roars the Führer. "Rome! Peenemünde!"

"Peenemünde?" asks Wünsche, as pale as a corpse.

"Peenemünde!" roars the Führer again. "Don't act so innocent. How did the English know we were building rockets there? From you, of course!"

"From me?" asks Wünsche, horrified.

"Who else?" the Führer yells. "I should have had you executed, for high treason. But I don't want to do that to Hansi. Canaris, take him to the concentration camp near Peenemünde. He belongs there, with his entire family!"

Canaris: *"Jawohl, mein Führer!"*

"And the dog?" stammers Wünsche in disbelief.

"He stays with me," says the Führer contentedly.

*

Sirius is now the personal dog of the Führer.

What a twist of fate. Should he be thankful for it? Sirius broods it over. It is an uncomfortable thought. The very man who poses the greatest threat to the world is now his protector.

On the other hand, if you have to go through hell, it's better to have the devil on your side. Or is even that no justification for a pact with the devil?

Sirius feels too small for such big questions. He just wants to survive.

The food—he won't deny it—is one of the advantages of life in the Führer's headquarters. For despite all the stories to the contrary, the Führer is by no means a strict vegetarian. He loves white sausage and game pie. He restricts himself from having too much of it, though, because he fears it will lead to flatulence. Ironically, the raw food he consumes in its place actually does lead to flatulence. It's a vicious cycle.

So the meat from the Führer's plate tends to end up in the dog bowl. That pleases the "doggy."

Sirius is playing the role of Hansi so well that Heinrich Hoffmann, the Führer's personal photographer, is brought onto the scene. The dog is a delightful motif, no doubt about it; he brings sunshine into the dark Reich Chancellery. At long last, Sirius is back in front of the camera, and he enjoys every moment.

Another advantage on the Führer's side is the bunker. When bombs rain down over Berlin—and that happens all through December—one can be oblivious to it in the subterranean quarters.

The dog is allowed in there too, of course. He lies at the Führer's feet. The closest military staff are there, as well as the servants. Everyone is lost in thought. Sirius thinks back to the nights when he was without shelter, wandering through the streets with bombs hailing down overhead. Now he has a roof over his head, and a concrete roof at that.

Each morning, following the night's air raids, bad news is delivered. The Kaiser Wilhelm Memorial Church is on fire, the Zoological Garden has been destroyed, the Kaufhaus des Westens no longer exists. By now, practically the entire city lies in ruins.

* * *

The English even bomb Berlin on Christmas Eve. The mood in the bunker is correspondingly bleak. Krause, the valet, is tying the Führer's cravat. Kempka, the chauffeur, is humming "Silent Night." Constanze Manziarly, the dietary chef, has decorated a little tree. It shakes whenever the ground tremors in the city above their heads.

The Führer stares grimly into space. His face doesn't even brighten when he opens his Christmas present from Joseph Goebbels: twelve Mickey Mouse films.

He says "Aha!" and Goebbels notes in his diary, "He was pleased and very happy with the treasure." But the truth is he's not happy. He wants the Final Victory. That would make him happy, and only that.

*

In Hollywood, it's time for the premiere of *Hercules and Cleopatra*.

The movie is so pitiful that the audience members indignantly set fire to their tickets after the showing and throw them back into the box office.

The critic from the *Hollywood Reporter* writes: "One finds oneself regretting that cars hadn't yet been invented in ancient Egypt. Or some other contraption that might be capable of running over dogs."

The critic of the *New York Times* says only "*Cave canem!*"

Carl Crown can't help feeling a certain Schadenfreude as he flicks through the papers and confirms that Sirius is still the King of Hollywood. His successor has failed miserably.

He pictures Jack Warner tearing his hair out in agitation. It turned out that Hercules really is irreplaceable.

But that's not the only reason why the family is keen to celebrate.

There is important news: Georg has American citizenship. He is now no longer a German, but an American.

A fitting celebration is called for. A table stands ready in Rondo, the restaurant in the Hilton Townhouse hotel.

The table is set for eight people. Carl, Rahel, Else, Andreas, Georg and Electra take their seats. Only the two surprise guests are still to arrive.

Then they come. Conrad Nicholson Hilton and Zsa Zsa Gabor in person. Zsa Zsa has her peach-colored Doberman pinscher, Caruso, under her arm.

"Daddy!" calls Electra, beaming with joy.

"Hello, sweetheart," replies Father Hilton with a smile, sinking down into a chair. It goes without saying that he is at the head of the table.

"Mister Hilton!" says Crown respectfully. The man is the leader of an army of Bordeaux-red-clad soldiers, after all, and Crown is one of them.

"Conny," corrects Hilton in a friendly tone.

He orders champagne for everyone. They all look at each other in surprise, apart from Georg and Electra, who are obviously in the know.

"Conny," says Georg, lifting his glass, "yesterday I asked for your daughter's hand . . ."

Electra giggles.

"You are the King of America," Georg continues. "I love your daughter and I want to marry her. You gave me your approval."

Everyone cheers. Rahel conceals her emotion behind a napkin.

Conrad Hilton towers up imposingly, just like one of his famous hotels in Manhattan.

"My grandmother's surname," he says, "was Laufersweiler. She was a simple woman from Dörebach, a farming village in the Hunsrück Mountains. German blood flows in our family's veins.

"But," he continues, slamming his fist down on the table, "Hitler has destroyed my German roots. Hitler is our enemy, and we must win this war!"

"Conny," Georg assures him courageously, "I swore to you that I would fight. For my love for your daughter, I will go to war. And when we have won the war, Electra and I will marry."

"Okay," replies Conny. "Be quick about it."

"Look after yourself!" warns Zsa Zsa.

The following day, Georg Crown reports as a voluntary military doctor with the Ninth Army of the U.S. forces in Europe.

*

The plight of the German troops is becoming increasingly bleak. On the Eastern Front, a catastrophe is looming: the army group there is in danger of collapsing, more than a million soldiers have already lost their lives, and the replacements are nothing but trembling children in uniform.

"Enough of this hopeless bloodshed!" demands Lieutenant General Bamler.

In the south, the Allies have already pushed forward to central Italy. The German army is retreating. The Battle of Monte Cassino rages.

In the west, Field Marshal Rommel is making all the necessary preparations for the opening of a new front. They are expecting the Allies to invade France.

The Führer is hoping for a miracle. Because only a miracle can save Germany now.

"What do the stars say?" he asks.

Heinrich Himmler feels as though the question is directed at him. Although you wouldn't think it to look at him, he is always all ears when the subject of mysticism comes up. He is known only as the austere SS commander who is responsible for the Final Solution, zealously trying to keep the gas ovens burning in the midst of war.

"The stars?" responds Himmler. "We would need to ask the astrologists for that. But none of them are alive anymore. On your orders, *mein Führer*, if I may remind you."

"Yes, yes." The Führer waves his hand dismissively. "And rightly so. They were poisoning the German people with their relentless pessimism. But who knows, maybe the stars have changed their minds."

"There was this one fellow," murmurs Himmler, as

though he is rummaging through his memory for the name. "Professor Wulff. I had him put in the Fühlsbuttel concentration camp. I'll check it out, maybe he's still alive."

Professor Wulff is still alive. And Himmler knows that very well, for he gets his horoscope from him once a month. He even sees to it that the astrologer is able to leave the camp under strict observation in order to perform his duties as an "academic employee" of the High Command of the Navy. Secretly, behind the Führer's back.

The High Command oversees a department whose role it is to detect enemy submarines with the help of supernatural forces. Psychics and prophesiers are employed there. Day after day, they circle their pendula over the sea maps. Astrology is used there too.

A short while later, Professor Wulff finds himself in the Führer's office. He is portly, elegantly dressed and wears a monocle. The Führer had imagined a concentration camp inmate to look a little bit more, well, miserable.

"You're keeping well, I see," says the Führer. Not for the first time, he is overcome by the uneasy feeling that he can't trust Himmler as far as he can throw him. But that is another matter.

"Thank you for asking," says the professor, seeking refuge in poetry. "'Called a star's orbit to pursue, What is the darkness, star, to you?' Nietzsche."

"A star's orbit, indeed," the Führer seizes his cue. "That's exactly what I wanted to talk to you about. Is the German Wehrmacht under a good star? What are the signs?"

The professor is well prepared. He rolls out the celestial chart, picks up the compass, circles it with dramatic movements over the planets, referring in particular to the lunar nodes, consulting the lines of latitude and historical data. He warns of Mars, offers encouraging news on Saturn.

Then the Führer interrupts. "Drop the hocus-pocus," he roars, "I just want to know one thing: Will we win the war?"

A difficult question. The astrologer knows, of course, that if he delivers bad news he will be punished with death; and if he delivers good news, he may be rewarded with his life. But either way, any prophecy will inevitably fall back on him as soon as it proves itself to be wrong. What to do?

Professor Wulff tries to buy himself some time.

"You have a new dog, don't you?" he asks.

The Führer is baffled. "How did you know that?"

Wulff points at the celestial chart and explains ceremoniously: "The Big Dog is in your zodiac sign. You can see it clearly, here is Sirius."

Sirius sticks his head out from under the desk, pricking up his ears at the sound of his name. Are they talking about him?

"You see!" calls the professor as he catches sight of the dog. "He hasn't just come into your life by accident. The stars wanted it that way. He's your fate."

"My fate?" asks the Führer.

"Indeed," responds the professor. "Even the ancient Egyptians listened to the warnings of Sirius. Whenever he appeared on the firmament, it was the sign for the annual flooding of the Nile. The Sumerians worshipped him as the

Wanderer of the Seas. He is a harbinger of danger from the water."

"The invasion in France!" guesses the Führer. "He's warning us!"

"He is indeed," confirms the professor.

"And?" asks the Führer anxiously. "Will there be a miracle?"

The professor takes out his monocle and peruses the celestial chart once more with even greater concentration.

"I see the signs of a miracle," he says.

"Where? Where?" the Führer demands to know.

"Here," says the professor, circling Mars with his finger. "It's in the constellation with Sirius. According to Ptolemy, that means mortal danger."

"For the Führer?" asks the Führer in shock.

"The gravest mortal danger," confirms the professor. "But as I said: I also see a miracle."

The Führer is crushed. He wavers between unbridled rage at the lowlifes who are after his blood, and heartfelt gratitude to the stars for warning him about it.

The astrologer, his head lowered, waits to discover which sentiment will ultimately win the upper hand.

He is in luck, and is ushered out. He mops the sweat from his brow with relief. He survived. It was also in the celestial chart that the Führer's days are numbered, to the very day even, but he stayed quiet about that.

The stars already know.

*

So now the focus is on war again, total war. Whenever the greatest field commander of all time has his hands full, he takes up residence in the Wolf's Lair. That's the name of the secret command headquarters in East Prussia, where "Wolf," as the Führer's friends call him, likes to hide away. With Sirius, of course.

The Wolf's Lair is anything but dog-friendly. For a start there is the six-mile-long barbed-wire fence which encloses the bunker town, and then the hundred-yard-wide mine field surrounding it.

The Führer and his doggy reside in Bunker No. 13.

"Take good care of Hansi!" the Führer orders his adjutant. "I don't want him to tread on a Teller mine while he's out for walkies."

"Yes, *mein Führer!*" replies the adjutant.

"That's what happened to Ribbentropp's dachshund," explains the Führer, imitating an exploding dog with his hands.

So Sirius is on his guard. Luckily there is enough to explore within the confines of the complex.

Within Exclusion Zone 3 are the barracks of the guard staff and the antiaircraft guns. Within Exclusion Zone 2 is the accommodation for the Wehrmacht command staff and the Führer's guard battalion.

Exclusion Zone 1, the "Führer Zone," is the most interesting. Here are the news headquarters, the officers' mess with its dining rooms, the camp barracks, the cinema, the Führer bunker, the hair salon and the residential bunkers of the leadership team; of Martin Bormann, leader of the

Chancellery, Reichsmarschall Göring, Field Marshal Wilhelm Keitel and so on.

SS guards stand at the gates to each exclusion zone. They check special identification documents and request the passwords which change on a daily basis. This doesn't apply to Sirius, of course. He is the Führer's personal dog, which gives him access to all areas, apart from the sauna.

It all reminds Sirius a little of the Warner Bros. studio city. The comparison may be slightly inappropriate, but Sirius is merely thinking of the many halls behind the barrier, the bustle of extras in their military costumes, the props, the canteen, the office bunker of the Hollywood mogul. As if this were a movie, *Hercules Against the Rest of the World*.

It's an unsettling thought. Is the deluded Führer playing the role of Hercules? Does he perhaps believe that the whole world is Luckyville and only he can save it?

By now, anything seems possible to Sirius. He sets off on his way to the canteen. Maybe fate will prompt a chicken bone to fall out of the window.

Two men come toward him. They stop and point.

"Look," says one.

"Yes, I see," says the other.

They step closer.

"Not bad," says one.

"Yeah, very good," says the other.

Sirius looks at them, wide-eyed.

For some reason, the scene seems familiar to him. Didn't his success in Hollywood begin with those very same words?

Could it be that they now spell bad luck? He is a superstitious dog.

The men walk off again. They are part of the planning staff in Barrack 99. There, fantastical ideas are being concocted for a completely new wonder weapon. The High Commander of the Army is becoming more and more desperate.

The prototype of a UFO, built in the Skoda factories, turned out to be a failure. So now there is a new plan: Why not fire dogs into the enemy lines? One would only need to inject them with the neurotoxin Tabun or Sarin, which would be released on impact and destroy everything in their vicinity. The production of expensive bombshells could then be dispensed with.

And this is what they want to try out on Sirius? Luckily, the news comes through just in time that he is the personal dog of the Führer.

Sirius goes to see what happens in the briefing barracks. The building is named as such because this is where the Führer is briefed on the current situation, and in fact this is happening right now. The map of the world is spread out on the huge table. Rommel is predicting an Allied invasion across the Strait of Dover, where the distance between France and England is the smallest. Jodl disagrees; he suspects that the landing will be in the south of France. One index finger after another pushes its way along the Atlantic Wall.

Sirius reflects on how wonderful it would be to be sitting at the piano right now. The Circle would take pleasure in every hint. How is the Circle doing, he wonders?

* * *

There is no need to worry. The Circle is still around. They were very concerned, of course, when the dog didn't turn up from one day to the next. But then his photo appeared in the newspaper, a snapshot by Heinrich Hoffmann, and they figured out the rest by themselves. In any case, Sirius is fit and well.

They miss the piano playing. But action is the priority now. There has to be a successful coup, and as soon as possible. No more procrastination. Even large sections of the Wehrmacht, the aristocracy and the administration are in agreement on that point. There are numerous "circles" by now. Their mission: to assassinate Adolf Hitler.

There is only one man for the job: Claus von Stauffenberg.

*

The Allied invasion is executed with a military force that the world has never seen before. The most powerful fleet of all time, six thousand ships, conquers the coast. The skies darken, the Luftwaffe open fire. Over the next few months, hundreds of thousands of soldiers storm onto land.

In Normandy. So not across the Strait of Dover, as Rommel predicted. The German troops have been thrown a red herring again, and need time to reorient themselves.

The world war is now raging in the very heart of Europe.

"Paris cannot fall into the hands of the enemy, and if it must, then only as a field of rubble!" commands Hitler. But his wish will not be fulfilled.

* * *

The liberators are on the advance, and wherever they march they are met by cheering French civilians, who hold uncorked red wine bottles high in their outstretched hands, inviting the soldiers to join them in a tipple. The girls blow kisses and cover the tanks with flowers. It's nice to be the liberator. In the west, that is.

In the east, the Red Army is drawing closer. They are already outside Lublin, in Poland. Here, the liberators are not met by cheers of joy. As they open the gates to Majdanek concentration camp, hell opens up before their eyes. More than a million Jews have been murdered here, their ashes still smoldering in the crematoria. The pictures of horror make their way around the world for the first time.

Berlin is still far away from both fronts, but the noose is growing tighter with every day that passes.

Dr. Georg Crown is stationed in the American marine hospital near Cherbourg, as a medical officer. Their main function is to provide emergency assistance. Bullet wounds, emergency amputations and so on. Everything has to happen quickly, life and death always hang in the balance. And the army of wounded is growing by the day.

But it's a small world, even in the midst of a world war. Dr. Crown steps up to the bed of a man who needs an urgent X-ray. He recognizes him at first sight—it's James Stewart, the Hollywood star.

"What are *you* doing here?" asks Crown.

"I escaped from a burning plane at the last minute," replies Stewart wearily. "With a parachute."

* * *

James Stewart is group operations officer of the 453rd Bombardment Group. He wears the Air Medal with oak leaf clusters, awarded for his aerial attacks on Germany.

"Your face seems familiar," says Stewart. "But where from?"

Crown thinks for a moment, rolling the bed over to the X-ray machine.

"I think you're confusing me with my father," he says. "I'm sure you know our dog, Hercules."

James Stewart smiles. "The dog, of course. Hercules, my greatest rival. What's he up to nowadays?"

"He's in Berlin," says Crown. "We don't know any more than that."

"In Berlin?" exclaims Stewart in surprise. "I was there too, but as a bomber up in the sky. Hopefully I didn't hit him." Then, with a wink, he adds: "What's that thing people say? You know, that our paths always cross twice in life."

The X-ray pictures give the all clear. Before long, James Stewart is climbing into the next available B-24.

"Say hello to Hercules from me, when you see him again," he calls out. "It surely won't be much longer now."

*

A major situation briefing in the Wolf's Lair. A discussion on the advance of the Red Army and to what extent blocking divisions should be used to seal off East Prussia. Colonel Claus von Stauffenberg, the man responsible for these matters from the military staff, has flown in especially from Berlin to make a report.

It is hot in the briefing barracks, so Stauffenberg asks for permission to go and freshen up. The Führer wrinkles his brow. He doesn't think it's that hot, and the other officers in the room aren't exactly fresh, either. But Field Marshal Keitel nods.

Stauffenberg comes back. He puts his briefcase down under the conference table, right next to Sirius. Sirius is surprised by the fact that the man is wearing an eye-patch, and that he's missing his right hand. Who does that remind him of? Oh yes, Barbarossa, the lion tamer. Maybe this man is a lion tamer too? His thoughts are just wandering to Benares, the lion, when he hears a gentle ticking in the briefcase.

The presentation is taking its time coming. Stauffenberg excuses himself again, this time saying that he needs to pop out to make a phone call. The Führer and Keitel are already leaning over the world map. The dog sniffs at the briefcase, and a strong smell rises into his nose. He gives a loud yelp.

"What's wrong, my doggy?" asks the Führer in concern. "Did I step on your paw?"

Alarich Heinzel, the Führer's adjutant, puts the briefcase somewhere else so that the dog has more space.

Then, all of a sudden, a deafening explosion rips through the room. The bomb in the briefcase has been detonated, and the shockwave is so powerful that it hurls Alarich Heinzel across to the window.

Then the ceiling caves in. Lieutenant General Rudolf Schmundt receives a blow to the head from a roof beam. The heavy map table splinters. Heinrich Berger, the stenographer, is killed on the spot, while the other men manage to crawl out into the open air, severely injured.

And the Führer?

With burst eardrums and tattered clothing, he staggers across the compound, clearly in shock. It is a miracle that he survived.

"It was destiny," he wheezes, covered in blood. "The stars wanted it that way."

Colonel General Jodl, also back on his feet, salutes: "*Mein Führer!* The miracle is called Hansi. If he hadn't yelped, the bomb would have exploded right next to you, and you would be dead."

"Hansi!" screams the Führer in desperation. "Where is my doggy?"

A search team clambers down into the ruins of the briefing barracks to find Hansi. The Gestapo, meanwhile, are hot on Stauffenberg's heels.

The dog lies buried beneath the map of the world. His heart is beating, but only weakly. His eyes are closed, peacefully, and his tongue hangs sideways out of his mouth.

Two men lift him carefully onto a stretcher. They cover him with the flag that was just on the table, as a mark of respect, and march off in goose step to his master.

Dr. Morell, the Führer's personal doctor, has been summoned. He inspects the dog thoroughly, listening to his chest with the stethoscope, checking his organs, shining a light through his pupils, measuring the temperature on his tongue—and then an expression of concern settles on his face.

The Führer is holding Hansi's paw. He is fighting back tears, and losing this battle too.

"Good doggy," he sobs, "you warned me."

Dr. Morell proceeds to the diagnosis: "A heart attack. The dog is critically ill."

The Führer commands: "Order to the Air Force! Fly Hansi to the Charité at once! Sauerbruch is to give it his all, I repeat, his all!"

The propellers can already be heard setting into motion. The dog opens his eyes briefly, seemingly with the very last of his strength, then immediately falls unconscious again when he meets the Führer's tear-soaked gaze.

The coup has failed. And it was all his fault.

*

Don't they say that a person's life flashes before their eyes in the very last seconds before they die? Well, exactly the same thing happens with dogs.

Sirius lies in the plane to Berlin, watching the palm trees on Sunset Boulevard rush past. He thinks of the visit to the dog cemetery that John Clark recommended. An honorary grave in Hollywood, side by side with Humphrey Bogart's dog. How wonderful that would be. He sees before him the widow who lives twice. Her gratitude makes him feel good. He remembers the meadows of Lucerne, and once again smells the wonderful scent of fresh manure.

Manzini waves at him. The magician is still standing in the circus ring, pointing with a shrug at the time machine and smiling wistfully, as if wanting to ask for forgiveness, as though he is saying: Even miracles can go wrong. Sirius understands completely. He too has just caused a miracle that wasn't how its creator intended it to be. He forgives the magician.

He has lived a wonderful, fulfilling life.

"Don't give up!" says the tree.

"I fear my time has come," breathes Sirius weakly.

"Oh, nonsense," replies the tree, "the next day is a new one."

Sirius pauses. "What do you mean by that?"

"*Gone With the Wind*," mumbles the tree, unsure now.

"Tomorrow is another day," says Sirius. "That's how it goes."

"Really?" says the tree in surprise. "Well, trees can't go to the cinema, remember."

Sirius tries to imagine a tree sitting in the cinema. The poor viewer behind him, only seeing the film through the branches. Missing the most important scenes because the trunk is in the way. The man gets up, goes to the box office and asks for his money back. They don't believe him, and accompany him back to the cinema, but by then the tree is already gone, because he didn't like the film.

Sirius falls into a peaceful sleep.

*

Professor Sauerbruch and the lead doctors are already standing at the ready when the dog arrives. He is driven up in the
state carriage. The Führer's guard battalion, which just this
once is now the Führer's dog's guard battalion, salutes.

"Patient Hansi!" announces the commander. "Emergency
case!"

The Charité is on red alert, as though the Führer himself
had been the victim of the explosion. Which, secretly,
Professor Sauerbruch would have preferred. He was a close
friend of Claus von Stauffenberg's; he even made his hand
prosthesis for him.

The dog is taken straight to the intensive care ward. He lies
on the table, hooked up to all kinds of devices and tubes. An
oxygen mask covers his snout. Thankfully, the monitor
reveals that he still has a heartbeat.

"Tension pneumothorax," diagnoses Sauerbruch. "Both
lungs have collapsed. Coronary vessels already severely
attacked. Critical condition. Don't x-ray, just take him
straight to the operating theater."

And yet Dr. Morell said it was a heart attack! He is
nothing but a charlatan. Everyone knows it; only the Führer
has remained loyal to him. He trusts the "miracle doctor"
blindly, eager for his daily "wonder injection." Exactly what
drugs are in it, only the devil knows. Methamphetamine or
cocaine, presumably. But that's another matter.

No one opens up a thorax better than Sauerbruch. It's
becoming his speciality. And it doesn't throw him in the
slightest that it's a dog's thorax, for he knows his stuff with

rib cages of all varieties. A lung is a lung. His main concern now is the patient's circulation—the dog's heart is beating weakly. On two occasions it even stops, and on the monitor only a straight green line can be seen, without any movement, deathly still. But then the pulse begins to beat again. Sirius is fighting for his life.

The operation draws out over a number of hours, and even the professor himself is at the very end of his strength when he finally lays down the scalpel.

"The dog has made it," he says. "He's going to survive."

At that very moment—and just a few streets away—Colonel General Fromm is giving a special commando the order to fire. Claus von Stauffenberg is executed on the spot. He dies with a cry of "Long Live Germany!"

*

Conrad Nicholson Hilton has invited Carl and Rahel Crown to his summer party, as the future parents-in-law of his daughter Electra. They have no idea that it will be their last big party in Hollywood, otherwise they would try to enjoy the evening more.

They are a little stiff and shy. The other guests know them, if at all, as hotel staff, dressed up in Bordeaux-red uniforms. Hilton introduces the Crowns as "friends of the family." When pressed for more information, he adds: "Mr. Crown is a famous Plato researcher from Berlin." Isn't that right? That's what his daughter told him, and she would know, because she's studying philosophy. In her twelfth semester.

* * *

"A porter who's a Plato scholar?" asks Rex Whittaker, the director of the New York Plaza Hotel, with a look of surprise. His wife looks piqued.

"Plato," she giggles tipsily, "isn't that the word doctors use for . . . ?" She points self-consciously at her husband's trouser fly.

"No, darling," replies Mr. Whittaker, adding in a whisper, "that's 'penis.'"

"Oh," she replies, rolling her eyes.

"Plato," Conrad Nicholson Hilton corrects, "was a philosopher in the Middle Ages."

The band plays "Bésame Mucho." People dance.

"Didn't you used to have a famous dog?" asks Rita Hayworth, who is now married to Orson Welles. "Goliath, or something like that?"

"Hercules," replies Crown.

Sad, but true. Hercules has slowly faded into obscurity in Hollywood. And the incompetent doppelgänger played a part in that. Jack Warner put the legend on ice.

"He's in Berlin," Rahel chips in. "On tour."

Rita Hayworth smiles sympathetically. "On tour? That's just another way of saying *Auf Wiedersehen*. Isn't it?"

"We hope so," says Crown, not catching her drift.

The Crowns don't mean to give themselves airs, but they now have a famous son-in-law. Andreas Cohn. He recently made his debut as a soloist, accompanied by the Los Angeles Philharmonic Orchestra. Mozart's Violin Concerto No. 3.

The *New York Times* enthused:

"We have listened to Menuhin. We have listened to Heifetz. We have listened to Oistrakh. Always with our ears. And now we have listened to Andreas Cohn. With our hearts."

The "Diablo," they call him. Because his virtuosity has almost demonic traits, but also because of his hellishly romantic looks. Women are throwing themselves at his feet.

"Didn't you bring the Diablo with you?" asks Lana Turner. "I'd love to hear how his violin sounds at close proximity. Very close proximity, if you know what I mean."

"Is it true that he thinks about Hitler while he's playing?" Ava Gardner wants to know. "I mean, during the angry parts."

"He doesn't think, he just feels," comments Crown knowingly.

"*Oh là là*," flirts Mae West. "Is that a violin in your pocket, or are you just pleased to see me?"

The band plays "As Time Goes By." People dance.

Then a man appears on the dance floor. He, too, just feels. He flings his arms upward, spins like a humming top, whirls like a dervish, and all to the sounds of a melancholy ballad. Oh yes, it's the funny Austrian with the cocked hat, Billy Wilder. He is hopping around in circles with Mrs. Whittaker.

"Hey, Crown," he calls, "long time no see. How are you?"

"He's a Plato scholar," Mrs. Whittaker whispers to the Austrian.

"Plankton," corrects Crown politely.

"Nobody's perfect," giggles the Austrian.

* * *

Electra is proudly wearing the war bride badge on her dress.

"Your husband is in the war?" asks John Wayne.

"My fiancé," responds Electra.

"Normandy?" asks Wayne.

"How should *I* know?" says Electra defiantly. "I'm not one of those women who constantly spy on their man. I don't have to know where he is and what he's doing all the time. I trust him."

"Of course." Wayne bows, retreating with a shake of his head.

Later, he sees Electra dancing with the young actor Freddie Winston, more closely than is appropriate for a woman whose fiancé is currently fighting in Normandy. Or wherever he is.

*

Sirius spends the entire summer in the Charité. And he enjoys it to the fullest. Professor Sauerbruch's private ward is luxurious in many ways; food from the Adlon Hotel, pretty nurses who could easily make a career in the movies, and much more. But the most important thing is this: here, one is in the care of the most famous medical practitioner in the world. Should—and the emphasis here is on "should"—something happen to someone here, then it wouldn't be down to human error, but fate. It is absolutely wonderful. All doubts are lifted, all fears, all ruminations, all dark thoughts. The heart is free. The mind is light. Life, otherwise such a trying affair, is carefree all of a sudden. As long as it lies in Sauerbruch's hands. Such a shame that one only gets to enjoy this when sick.

The artist Jobst Korthe, another of the professor's patients, put this into words very beautifully. He often engages the dog in the neighboring room in conversation.

"Look," he says, "this is my tube of black paint. I haven't used it one single time since I've been here. Before I used to get through twenty tubes a week."

Sirius likes the paintings. Expressionism, presumably. Korthe sits at the easel and paints what he sees when he looks out of the window. And it's true; even the bridge over the Spree, which really is black, looks green in the picture.

"I would love to paint your portrait one day, Master Hansi," says Korthe. He addresses the dog formally. Only Sauerbruch calls everyone by their first names.

And so Sirius sits for the painter. *Dog before Berlin*, the picture is to be titled. The dog takes up his position on the windowsill.

What does it remind him of? He has to think for a long while. Then the glass house comes into his mind. Villa Hercules. "When Hercules sits by the window, his silhouette will become one with the backdrop of the city," Miss Green had rejoiced. Was that her name, Miss Green?

Strange that his silhouette always ends up becoming one with the backdrop of the city, regardless of where he is.

Lost in thought, he stares out of the window. How desolate Berlin looks. Entire areas of the city lie in ruins. The charred Kaiser Wilhelm Memorial Church towers up from the gray sea of houses like a hollow tooth. With this view, one needs to be an Expressionist to get away with leaving the black paint untouched.

There is a knock at the door, and Professor Sauerbruch steps in.

"Korthe!" he exclaims. "You're supposed to be in bed, not painting!"

He surveys the artwork on the easel. He even pulls his glasses out of his breast pocket. "Have you no eyes in your head? Where on earth is this building in Berlin, this yellow tower here?"

"It's not in Berlin, Herr Professor, it's in my imagination," says Korthe, beaming.

"Ahah," says Sauerbruch. "And the red glove? Or what is that?"

"The dog," responds Korthe, offended.

"The dog," murmurs Sauerbruch with a shake of his head. "Well, just don't show that picture to Hitler, or you're a dead man."

"No, no," stammers Korthe, "I'm in so-called inner emigration."

Then Sauerbruch turns to Sirius. "Speaking of Hitler, the Führer called me. He wants to know if you are better at last, and I answered truthfully. You will be discharged tomorrow morning."

Sirius whimpers in shock.

"I'm sorry," says Sauerbruch. "You were our ray of sunshine here. We'll miss you on the ward."

He looks into the dog's sad eyes. "Good-bye, little red glove. Look after yourself."

*

The Red Army has already advanced into East Prussia, a hefty blow. The Wolf's Lair had to be evacuated, and the headquarters are now in the Berlin Chancellery once more.

Sirius is horrified when he sees the Führer again. The man is a shadow of his former self. He walks hunched over and has become old. His left arm and left leg shake. His face, too, is contorted with pain from the relentless colic. He is almost blind in his right eye.

It's unfathomable, thinks the dog, that hosts of armies from all over the world are needed to free the world from this geriatric.

The Führer doesn't even have the energy to bend over to his doggy and greet him.

"There you are," he mumbles, "welcome back."

Dr. Morell is now constantly by his side. The effect of the last "wonder injection" barely has time to fade before he administers the next. Then the dark mood lifts momentarily, and for a brief moment the Führer regards his final victory to be possible again.

"Only his iron will is keeping him on his feet now," whispers Goebbels, full of amazement.

Field Marshal Model and Colonel General Jodl arrive for a situation report. They bring depressing news.

"I've had enough of the never-ending defensive!" rants the Führer.

He means the Western Front, which is surrendering more ground with every passing day. The Allies have already reached the Rhine. The Rhine! Another few miles, thinks Hitler, and the Lorelei will be in their hands.

The Führer commands the offensive and christens it Operation Watch on the Rhine. It must be a battle which brandishes an iron fist to the enemy.

All of the Wehrmacht's reserves are to be mobilized. It is all or nothing now. The annihilation of the Allies, or the end.

The attack begins on December 16, at the stroke of 5:30 A.M. The Führer himself trudges to the Adlerhorst command post on the front, in order to give the annihilating blow the highest authority.

But after just a week, the attack collapses. The army from the west is too powerful and the attackers hopelessly inferior, the majority of them children in uniform or doddery old men with helmets.

In the middle of the Ardennes, a brave farmer's wife is the harbinger of approaching peace. On Christmas Eve, she positions herself between the troops and coaxes both sides to lay down their arms and forget the war for a few hours. Singing German and English Christmas songs, the soldiers celebrate together late into the night.

*

The Führer returns to Berlin. He is bitterly disappointed by the German men on the front. They were too weak. Lacking in iron will. Toward the end of his days, it dawns on the Führer that the fault lies with the German people; they didn't prove themselves to be worthy.

He moves one last time, now into the bunkered Führer apartment in the cellar of the Reich Chancellery. He suspects that this will be his final destination.

The apartment is small, and not just by the standards of the greatest Führer of all time; even a community gardener would feel cramped in here. The room for the situation briefings—which admittedly an allotment gardener wouldn't need—measures exactly twelve square yards. The walls are damp because the bunker lies beneath ground-water level. A mass of pumps siphon off the rivulets. Glaring bulbs provide the only light. Thick iron doors seal the air. It is stuffy, and it stinks.

There sits the commander, not knowing where to direct his rage. Constanze Manziarly, the dietary chef, serves him his beloved muesli.

"What is this?" he barks at her. "I can't stand to see this gruel anymore!"

"But think about your gut," pleads the cook, bursting into tears.

And so what? Warsaw is gone. Aachen too. Auschwitz has been liberated. Vienna is teetering on the brink. What does flatulence matter now?

Albert Speer, the Minister of Armaments, comes to visit and finds a broken man before him.

"If we lose the war," says the Führer, "then the people will be lost too. The German people have proved to be the weaker."

"Now come on, don't give up on our noble soil just yet," advises Speer.

"The soil?" rages the Führer. "Oh, no. There won't be any soil left, either."

"Why not?" asks Speer.

"Because," bellows the Führer with the last of his strength, for he has asthma now too, "because I am giving the order: Burn the land! Destroy everything! The enemy will end up wondering what kind of land they have conquered. A barren, worthless land."

"And the German people?" stammers Speer.

"—Should be given no more consideration!" orders the Führer. "They will survive in the most primitive of ways. That is their fate."

Speer leaves the cellar, shaking his head.

He is not the only stalwart to turn his back on the Führer at this time. Heinrich Himmler has, on his own initiative, made contact with Dwight D. Eisenhower, the commander in chief of the Allied Forces in Europe. He offers unconditional surrender, just like that, as though Adolf Hitler doesn't even have a say in it anymore. Eisenhower, a man of shrewd mind, passes on the message to the press, and the Führer finds out about it. Outraged, he immediately expels Himmler from all his posts.

Hermann Göring has retreated to the mountainside retreat of Obersalzberg. In the shadow of the Berghof, he composes a telegram to the Führer in which he boldly proclaims himself as successor, with all powers, unless the message arrives by 10 P.M. that the Führer is prepared to leave Berlin. The message doesn't arrive, but at around the hour in question, Göring is arrested.

Only Goebbels and Bormann stay loyal to the Führer. They are now living alongside him in the cramped bunker apartment. Goebbels has brought his family along as reinforcements: his wife, Magda, and their six children.

The children are supposed to cheer up "Uncle Adolf." An absurd plan, particularly when it leads to them filling his bathtub up with water and crashing around in it noisily. In all likelihood, this probably contributed to his suicidal thoughts.

Since the end of March, Eva Braun has been living in the subterranean community too. She has always dreamed of being the official wife of the Führer, but unfortunately he has always been married to Germany.

And right in the thick of all this is the dog.

"Hansi," calls the Führer, when he sits there in the armchair at night, alone, brooding to himself. Who else is willing to lend him their ear so patiently? In the glow of the lightbulb, the former field commander reminisces on his greatest triumphs, describing the front lines of years gone by, wallowing in the memories. Sometimes he cries uncontrollably.

The doggy has sympathy for the sick, old man whose world is falling apart. Sirius hates Hansi for this, and Hercules in turn would love to pounce up at the old man's throat and get revenge for Levi. Are they not all one and the same dog? The dog will have to be careful, otherwise he might lose his mind.

And he's not the only one.

But that's how it is right now, in this bunker. It's hard to

PART 3

tell who will lose their mind first, or even whether the
person in question was ever in their right mind in the first
place.

Like Dr. Goebbels, for example. When the bombs hail
down on the ground, which in the bunker is essentially the
ceiling, he calls his wife and children to him, and then they
sing in unison at the top of their voices:

"The blue dragoons, with beating drums,
through the gates they come.
The fanfare is their guide,
As high up the hillside they ride."

In reality, though, it's not quite like that. Two million
Red Army soldiers are before the gates of Berlin, the army
of tanks already rolling in. The sky is black with warplanes,
and their bombs are transforming the city into a field of
rubble. Berlin is sinking into ruins and ashes.

*

One evening in April, master and dog are sitting faithfully
together when the Führer says solemnly:

"Hansi, the time has come. We are to marry."

The dog gives a start. What? Now the Führer wants to
marry him too? Just what he needs!

"Be my best man," asks the Führer, his voice trembling
with emotion.

Hansi nods, relieved.

* * *

Shortly after midnight, municipal officer Walter Wagner appears, the registrar. Eva Braun is wearing a pretty dark blue dress with a white ruched collar. The Führer appears in a gray suit. Together with the two witnesses, Goebbels and Hansi, the couple stride toward their marriage ceremony.

The groom is a widower. His first wife was called Germany. Now he is daring to venture into married life once more.

So now there is also a widower who lives twice. Should Sirius give a warning growl? He restrains himself from doing so.

The ceremony is short and succinct. Tyrone Chester, the King of Heartstring Pulling, would have made more of it, no question.

The following day, the newlywed Hitlers host a lunch, for which the dietary chef and both secretaries are warmly invited to join them at the table. They have leek soup.

The conversation is drowned out again and again by artillery fire, which they can hear through the air shafts. The Russians are already hoisting the Soviet flag on the Reichstag, and they could storm the bunker any minute now.

Herr and Frau Hitler do the rounds one last time, proffering a handshake to every single person in farewell, accompanied by a few personal words.

The good-bye with his doggy proves to be the hardest for Hitler. "What will become of you when I'm no longer here?" he asks in concern.

* * *

PART 3

The dog has no idea. His entire life has always hung on a thread, and that thread was always connected to this man.

What Levi was, what Sirius is, what Hansi became—all of it was just a consequence, an escape, an act of providence.

He doesn't know what will be left of him when Hitler is no longer there.

The master and dog take their farewell. Their fates were always intertwined in mythical ways, and in the end their paths even crossed in reality.

The Hitlers withdraw to the living room. Adjutant Heinzel closes the door with the words: "They don't want to be disturbed now."

Then a gunshot is heard. And if the Red Army wasn't being so loud, maybe the biting of the cyanide capsule would be audible too.

That was the end.

*

And the beginning. The zero hour.

On May 8, all of London cheers Winston Churchill as he appears on the balcony of Buckingham Palace with the royal family and stretches his hand out into the victory sign. In Paris, the bells of all the cathedrals toll. "The war is won!" cries General de Gaulle at the Arc de Triomphe, and the people break out into a delirium of joy. In Moscow, Stalin congratulates his people: "From now on, the great banner of freedom and peace will wave over Europe!" In New York, a replica of the Statue of Liberty stands in Times Square, almost to scale, surrounded by the thunderous applause of the crowd.

And in Berlin?

A ghostly silence lies over the city as Sirius steps back onto the street for the first time. It is so quiet that he gives a start when a drop of water frees itself and falls onto a corrugated iron sheet.

Entire sections of the city have been burned down to their foundations. Here and there, a building's skeleton protrudes out of the field of rubble with an almost helpless air, as if it were wondering why it still exists.

In the middle of the street, a man leans over a dead horse. He is in the process of cutting it up for food. The animal is still steaming. With his bare hands, the man throws everything edible into a wheelbarrow, looking around repeatedly to make sure there is no one nearby with whom he would have to share his precious loot.

Sirius can still hear the creaking of the wheelbarrow even once he has reached the next crossing. Is he himself precious loot? The thought sends a shiver down his back. It is probably better to avoid humans under the present circumstances. Hunger is unscrupulous.

He finds it difficult to orient himself in the rocky wasteland. In many parts, the streets are no longer recognizable. Piles of rubble stand in his path, higher than the ruins which were once houses. Sometimes, voices can be heard in the ruins. The people are hiding, through fear of the Russians.

PART 3

Sirius walks through the Brandenburg Gate, which is still standing. Only one column has been shot to pieces.

Red Army tanks are posted on both sides of the gate. One of the guard soldiers opens his trouser fly demonstratively to relieve himself on the historic landmark. The others cheer him on. A bottle of vodka is passed around, not the first.

Sirius walks on, straight down the Charlottenburg Chaussee. Where is he going? Even he doesn't really know. Where one wants to go is often a puzzle anyway, and every once in a while the mystery is solved once one arrives there. Or not. Isn't that how it is?

A small dog in a big city, where not a single stone has been left standing. He stomps bravely through the debris. Street signs that could help point the way no longer exist. No church tower, no Kaufhaus des Westens, no kiosk. Everything is just a great emptiness, and the wind whistles through it.

Maybe he has even been walking down a familiar street for a while now, but how would he know? Where there are no more houses, the streets disappear too. Where there is no more life, the world becomes gray and uniform. One ruin looks just like the next.

Isn't that Frau Zinke?

A woman is sweeping the street. There is no one else to be seen far and wide, just rubble and ashes.

She drops the broom, dumbfounded, as she catches sight of the dog.

* * *

"Now isn't this a surprise!" she says. Her brow wrinkles, clearly she is thinking hard. "Sirius! Isn't that right?"

Sirius gives a start.

"Your name has changed so often," she grumbles, "it's very confusing, you know."

She carries on sweeping. "Things have to be kept in order," she says.

Sirius looks around. So this is Klamtstrasse. This used to be his home. Parts of the house in which he used to live are still standing. The facade has collapsed, otherwise he would have recognized it straightaway. On closer inspection, remnants of the ceiling frieze can be made out, the very fragment in which Adam is pointing his finger at his creator.

Frau Zinke is now sweeping the individual pieces of rubble.

Sirius studies her attentively. Has Frau Zinke been freed now? Is the day of emancipation a happy one for Frau Zinke? Have the Allied armies done Frau Zinke a favor? Have 50 million people died so that Frau Zinke can finally sweep in peace?

Klamtstrasse is desolate, no longer a street, just a swath between mountains of rubble and isolated house skeletons. In front of them, here and there, a charred tree trunk still stands.

Only now does Sirius notice. Where are the mighty trees which used to transform the street every spring into a lush green garden walkway?

Only one single tree is still standing.

* * *

Sirius approaches it hesitantly.

"Hello?" he whispers.

"Yes," says the tree. "It's me."

"Thank God!" rejoices the dog, "for a minute there I thought they got you."

"Likewise," smiles the tree.

"I have to . . ." says the dog, lifting his leg.

"Of course," replies the tree. "Make yourself at home."

Sirius pauses. "At home?"

"Well, you are at home now," says the tree. "The war is over, and soon everything will be like it was before."

"Is that what you really believe?" says the dog.

"It's what I hope," answers the tree.

The wind blows a cloud of dust through the air. Frau Zinke picks up her broom and sweeps.

"Give it a rest, Frau Zinke," calls the neighbor. "It's no good."

To the dog, he hisses quietly: "Old Zinke, first her husband fell in Stalingrad, then she lost both her sons in the militia at the very end. They were just children. Since then she's gone completely mad."

*

There's nothing to keep the Crowns in Hollywood anymore. Now that—in the words of President Truman—the flags of freedom are waving over Europe, the family feels drawn back to their home. Back to Berlin. Back to Sirius.

The images of the destroyed city are a shock, of course.

"Where are these flags supposed to be waving from?" asks Carl in disbelief. "I mean, there's not one single mast still standing." But as everyone knows, flags of freedom don't need masts; they wave in thoughts, in words, on the Sabbath.

An aerial photograph shows the ruins of Charlottenburg. "There!" cries Rahel in agitation, "I think I can see our house!" Her trembling index finger traces the path that Sirius trotted down.

"Sirius is somewhere there among the rubble," she sighs. "He's waiting for us."

Carl takes out his magnifying glass. Isn't it strange how objects from the past take on greater meaning as soon as homesickness is involved? The magnifying glass. It has slumbered in the drawer for so long. There was no use for it in Hollywood; things were already big enough here.

He leans over the picture, fixing his gaze on a tiny white fleck which could just as easily be a speck of dust. The emphasis being on "could," for perhaps it really is Sirius.

"I'm sensing," he says with a smile, "that my eyes are longing for the invisible once more."

He is still wearing the Bordeaux-red uniform with the gold bobbles, which doesn't exactly punctuate the deeper meaning of his words. He is, without a doubt, the only German in uniform who is going home without guilt.

Fate probably has a hand in it when two letters arrive from Berlin. One of them, with numerous stamps suggesting a great many detours during its journey, is addressed to Professor Carl Liliencron.

Dear Herr Professor,
The Board of Directors of the Prussian Academy of
Sciences has today been newly constituted. It would be
our honor to welcome you as a member of the academy
and as honorary professor of plankton research within
the faculty.
Signed, President of the Academy, Professor P. Seewald.

The second letter, addressed to the Los Angeles Philharmonic, is opened by Andreas Cohn.

Dear Herr Cohn,
On the 26th of May the Berlin Philharmonic will give
its first postwar concert in Berlin. Mendelssohn
Bartholdy's "A Midsummer Night's Dream Overture."
A momentous occasion which we hope will move you
to consider joining our orchestra as first violinist, for
this date and beyond.
Regards, Leo Borchard.

Two men in luck. Their exile has come to an end. And
Korngold turned out to be right: Mendelssohn did survive
Hitler.

Conrad Nicholson Hilton responds to the Crowns' plans for
their future with a frown: "What?" he stutters. "You want
to go back to the Stone Age?"

"The Stone Age," replies Crown, "was actually the time
when the Neanderthals became *Homo sapiens*. Now we

want to do our part to make sure that the miracle repeats itself."

Hilton isn't sure that he really understands this, but he senses that there is something celebratory in the air, and allows himself to be moved to a grand gesture:

"You'll fly Pan American!" he cries.

The airline has recently announced that from now on there will be direct flights from New York to Europe. The Hilton family has been invited onto the inaugural flight. So instead, the Crown family is given the honor.

Conrad Nicholson has ulterior motives, of course, otherwise he wouldn't be Conrad Hilton. He is not exactly unhappy about the fact that the Crowns want to disappear from the picture so swiftly. His daughter Electra has changed her mind, and now wants to marry that young actor Freddie Winston.

Bad luck for Georg. He went to war especially for Electra, and now he is coming home empty-handed. Electra's letter of farewell is already on its way. A delicate subject, which the bride's father would rather discreetly circumnavigate.

He asks casually: "How is Georg doing?"

"Good," replies Crown. "His unit is stationed on the Elbe. I think it will be a while before we see him in Berlin. After all, Berlin is still occupied by the Russians."

"Ah yes, the Russians," murmurs Hilton. "Ivan and that lot."

It reassures him to hear that the spurned fiancé is at a safe distance.

"Right then," he says, eager to wrap up the conversation. "All the best in Berlin, Crown!"

In the hotel lobby, Crown runs into John Clark. "No red bobble hat today?" asks Clark.

"No, not anymore," replies Crown, and this time he beats his old friend to it: "Let's go and have a drink!"

"One last one," he adds.

Clark looks at his watch in surprise. "The last one? How many have you already had? It's only midday."

"The last one ever," replies Crown, telling him the news.

"No way!" declares Clark. "Well then, first you need to say a proper good-bye to Hollywood."

They race down Sunset Boulevard in Clark's convertible together, back into the past.

"My name is Carl Liliencron," says Clark, imitating the newcomer.

Crown retaliates with memories of his time as a guardian angel in the Banana House.

"Do you remember how we drove through Hercules's handcuffs on Hollywood Boulevard?" asks Clark.

"Of course," says Crown, "I'll miss that in Berlin."

"Good luck there!" laughs Clark.

"I'm wilder than the West, and that's a fact!" cries Crown.

Such crazy years.

In the Formosa, they order a round of gin fizzes. And another. And another. And another. And another.

The next day, when Carl Crown climbs into the airplane with his family, it is not just the flag of freedom waving, but the flag of the Formosa too.

*

In May, there are days when Berlin is already skipping ahead into summer, and it's beautifully warm. Today is one of those days.

The sky shines its brightest blue, even though it is arched over a city that lies in ruins.

Sirius wanders through the streets, feeling hungry. It's not easy to find something edible when all the humans' stomachs are rumbling too. On every corner, there is someone exchanging something for something that can be eaten. Sirius watches as a packet of cigarettes and a stack of turnips change hands. A turnip, that would be just the ticket right now. His mouth waters. He pushes his way into the bartering process by sitting up and begging, and puts on his best irresistible expression.

"Get lost!" curses the man who has just taken ownership of the turnips. "I need these to feed my family. For an entire week."

Sirius scampers away. He makes his rounds for a while longer, then gives up. He lies down on a patch of grass that is catching the rays of sunshine.

"Do you have to lie right where I want to sweep?" scolds Frau Zinke. She brandishes her broom threateningly.

* * *

A Jeep with an American flag drives past. The hood is up and a large movie camera is jutting out of it.

"Stop!" calls the cameraman. He films Frau Zinke sweeping the ruins.

"A widow always sweeps twice," laughs the director on the Jeep's crossbar, shaking his head in disbelief.

Sirius can't believe his eyes. He knows these men. The one behind the camera is Tyrone Chester. The other is the strange Austrian with the cocked hat, Billy Wilder.

Tyrone Chester sees the dog in the sunshine, framed by the ruins, and his foolproof sense for tear-jerking scenes tells him that this is a fantastic motif. It would be even more powerful, of course, if the dog were lying not on the grass, but on the rubble and ashes.

Sirius senses what is required of him, and positions himself poignantly on the rubble and ashes. He doesn't want to seem like a know-it-all, but wouldn't it be even more moving if he were to whimper softly too?

"Fantastic!" calls Chester. "He's whimpering softly. That really tugs at the heartstrings."

Then, all of a sudden, he frowns. "Just a minute," he murmurs. "Isn't that Hercules?"

"No, it's Sirius," corrects Frau Zinke.

"Exactly," replies Chester. "Hercules!"

The dog waves his tail cheerfully and barks in greeting. He nestles up against the man who discovered him. Twice, one should say now. First in Hollywood, and now in Berlin.

"Hercules!" rejoices Chester. "Welcome back to Hollywood!"

Frau Zinke doesn't understand the world anymore. "So now he has another new name," she grumbles. "Today he's called this, and the next day something else."

"Nobody's perfect," giggles Billy Wilder.

Frau Zinke has had enough of the disruption. She needs to carry on sweeping.

"What are you doing here anyway?" she asks.

"Colonel Wilder," says her conversation partner by way of introduction. "Officer of the U.S. Army, film department. We've been on location in Auschwitz, Dachau, Bergen-Belsen, Buchenwald. Places that you probably don't know anything about."

"No." Frau Zinke shakes her head.

"Then you are exactly our target group," says Wilder. "The film is called *Death Mills*. In movie theaters from October. Definitely worth seeing."

"I don't have time," says Frau Zinke, picking up her broom and disappearing down into her cellar.

Sirius shakes off the rubble and ash from his fur. Okay, so it was just a short scene, a minor role, but he did a great job. Not bad after his career setback. And now Hollywood is calling.

"Come with us!" calls Chester. "We're flying back tonight. Jack Warner won't believe his eyes: Hercules, the Return!"

* * *

Sirius hesitates. Here he stands, just a few steps away from the house where he lived before he had to take flight. How often has he longed to be back here? Wasn't coming home the point of his long journey?

"Get in!" calls Billy Wilder. "What's holding you back?"

He's right, thinks Sirius. His home is now nothing but a pile of bricks. What's left for him here?

"You're unsure?" asks the tree.

"Yes," admits Sirius.

"So I see," says the tree. "You no longer know where home is."

Sirius nods.

"I'm going to tell you something," says the tree. "Home is the wherever your heart is."

"My heart?" asks Sirius.

"Yes," says the tree. "Where is your heart at home?"

"With the people I love," says Sirius.

"So there you have it," says the tree. "You have found your home, after all. Now your home just has to find you."

"I don't understand," says Sirius.

"Just wait," says the tree.

It's strange how the tree always speaks in riddles, Sirius grumbles to himself. His head is spinning. But for some reason he feels cheerful, his gloomy mood has lifted. His heart suddenly leaps. And when your heart leaps, you have to follow it, he thinks, rushing off.

"Where are you going?" Billy Wilder calls after him. "Come with us!"

Sirius turns around briefly, shakes his head, wags his tail in farewell and barks his own version of *Auf Wiedersehen.*

Then he makes his way back to the patch of grass. The sun is no longer shining, but the grass is still warm. He stretches out and closes his eyes. Perhaps my home will find me here, he ponders.

Sirius decides to just wait.

*

Klamtstrasse is a desolate sight. The wind whistles through the hollow houses, sucking the ash from the ruins and spitting it out again in disgust, as though it were coughing.

The clouds of smoke gradually drift away to reveal some figures approaching in the distance. There are four . . . no, five of them. The smaller one seems to be a child.

Their footsteps are weary. They are lugging heavy suitcases. Every few feet they stop, look around searchingly, point at this or that, and then venture forward a little more. It is the Liliencron family.

They get closer and closer. The child runs ahead, stopping by each ruin and calling out: "Is this where we live?"

The Liliencrons are coming back. The sight of the devastated city brings tears to their eyes. Only now, seeing their once familiar street in ruins, do they sense that this is not a homecoming in the truest sense of the word. It is a return to a place where their home no longer stands.

"Look, a man!" calls the little boy.

A man steps onto the street. He looks like a ghost. He was actually on his way to the black market at the Brandenburg Gate, to turn his watch into a shaving kit. Then his gaze falls on the new arrivals. He freezes in shock.

"Uncle Benno!" cry the Liliencrons in chorus, rushing to embrace him. Uncle Benno buries his face in his hands. He doesn't know whether to cry with joy or laugh with despair.

"Welcome to Berlin!" he sobs.

He can't bear to watch the family standing in front of their house, which used to be an elegant town house but is now just ash and rubble.

"Is this our new home?" asks the little boy.

"Yes," says Rahel. "But we have to build it up again first."

"Come on, Johnny, let's make a start right away," calls Else, as if it were a child's game.

She takes a stone from the huge mountain of rubble, eyes it carefully from all angles, then puts on an expression of wonder: "I wonder where *this one* belongs?"

Johnny thinks carefully. "Up there, on the roof!" he decides. "Put it on the roof, Papa!"

Andreas feigns outrage: "You two can't just take a stone from Uncle Benno's stone collection like that. He went to a great effort to gather them all together. You'll have to ask for his permission first."

Uncle Benno frowns dramatically, as though he is struggling with his emotions on the matter, but eventually gives his approval.

Then Carl takes charge, and solemnly lays the stone on the ground.

"This is the foundation stone," he says. "It is the symbol of our homecoming. The foundation for our future."

They all stare at the stone, mesmerized.

"Now all that's missing is Sirius," sighs Rahel.

"Sirius!" calls Johnny. He yells, screams even, at the very top of his lungs, so loud that the dog could even hear his name if he were on the other side of the city. "Sirius!"

Frau Zinke comes out of her cellar, looking perturbed.

"What's all this noise?" she mutters.

At the sight of the Liliencrons, something resembling shock flashes in her eyes. Or maybe it is shame. Or just conjunctivitis from all the sweeping.

She thinks hard for a moment, and then she remembers: "Liliencron! Professor Liliencron."

"We're looking for our dog," says Liliencron.

Frau Zinke looks around, puzzled. "Strange," she says, "he was here just yesterday."

Professor Liliencron can't believe his ears. Is he mistaken, or can he hear barking in the distance? Barking aimed at him?

A sound so familiar that his heart contracts. No, he's not mistaken.

There's only one dog who barks like that, and his name is Sirius.

Good old Sirius. He thought long and hard about what the tree must have meant. Now your home just has to find you. And he has been barking ever since, without pause. After all, what else can he do to make sure that his home finds him?

He barks to the point of exhaustion, certain that, at some point, his home will come back and find him.

Suddenly he hears a voice calling his name. He gives a start and runs off. He runs as quickly as he can. The street is long, four legs are too few, and he wishes he could run even faster. "I'm coming!" he barks.

He runs past his tree.

"Sorry, but I don't have time to chat," he wheezes. "They're here!"

"I know," smiles the tree. "They're waiting for you."

Sirius is happy. He runs and runs until he falls into the outstretched arms of his family, crumpling in exhaustion.

His home has found him at last.

ABOUT THE AUTHOR

Jonathan Crown was born in Berlin in 1953 and has since led a nomadic life, not unlike Sirius, the hero of his first novel. So far, his travels have taken him to Zurich, New York, Saint-Paul de Vence and Sorrento. A fox terrier named Louis was his companion for all these journeys. Crown is now back in Berlin, where he lives with his dachshund, Kelly.

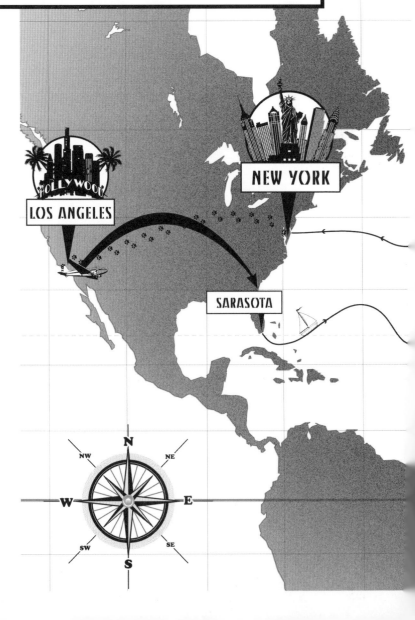